LOVE
IS
NO
SMALL
THING

YELLOW SHOE FICTION
Michael Griffith, Series Editor

LOVE
IS
NO
SMALL
THING

STORIES

MEGHAN KENNY

LOUISIANA STATE UNIVERSITY PRESS
BATON ROUGE

Published with the assistance of the Borne Fund

Published by Louisiana State University Press
Copyright © 2017 by Meghan Kenny
All rights reserved
Manufactured in the United States of America
First printing
LSU Press Paperback Original

Designer: Barbara Neely Bourgoyne
Typeface: Livory
Printer and binder: LSI

Library of Congress Cataloging-in-Publication Data
Names: Kenny, Meghan, 1974– author.
Title: Love is no small thing : stories / Meghan Kenny.
Description: Baton Rouge : Louisiana State University Press, 2017. |
Series: Yellow shoe fiction
Identifiers: LCCN 2016041523 | ISBN 978-0-8071-6626-0 (pbk. : alk. paper) |
ISBN 978-0-8071-6627-7 (pdf) | ISBN 978-0-8071-6628-4 (epub) |
ISBN 978-0-8071-6629-1 (mobi)
Subjects: | GSAFD: Love stories.
Classification: LCC PS3611.E6687.A6 2017 | DDC 813/.6—dc23
LC record available at https://lccn.loc.gov/2016041523

The paper in this book meets the guidelines for permanence and durability of the Committee on Production Guidelines for Book Longevity of the Council on Library Resources. ⊚

For my parents, John and Patricia Kenny

But the law of loving others could not be
discovered by reason, because it is unreasonable.

∾

Leo Tolstoy, *Anna Karenina*

CONTENTS

LOVE
IS
NO
SMALL
THING

LOVE IS NO SMALL THING

It was Halloween night and I was dressed as a 1980s prom queen—white satiny dress with a diagonal hem, bangs sprayed hard as a rock and feathered like a tidal wave, light-blue eyeliner and zinc-pink lipstick. I didn't look hot. Val was Jimmy Connors, in tight white terrycloth shorts and an Izod polo, terrycloth wristbands, a black bowl-cut wig, and a cheap Prince racket he found at the Youth Ranch. We drank peach schnapps and vodka and were fuzzy warm from the booze and from jumping around to Men at Work in honor of my costume. We were waiting for our friend Tim to call to let us know where to meet for the night.

"Jenni," Val said, "do the construction sweep, darlin'." This was my dance move, where I stopped traffic with one hand and redirected in a grand sweep with the other. We did the construction sweep for minutes, and then Val started swatting my ass with his racket.

"Lob," he said. "This Prince and your sweet butt make for a good lob."

Val and I had fun together. I loved him, and hoped we'd get married and have a baby and live our lives together in his little bungalow in Boise's North End. But after three years of dating, I was weary of waiting for him to decide if I was someone he wanted. I was thirty-five and he was thirty-eight. How long did we have to wait? What is it in us that keeps hope? That makes us think *maybe, just maybe* something will change?

I TAUGHT FOURTH-GRADERS reading and writing at a rural public school in southern Idaho. Most of the kids were first-generation Mexicans or South Americans. Their parents came to the land of opportunity, came to plant and harvest and haul onions and sugar beets and potatoes in this part of the country. They lived in migrant camps and were poor, but didn't know they were poor. Not in Wilder, Idaho. Some had come from California; some were born in Idaho. Some had been to California or Mexico to visit, but hardly anyplace else. Sometimes they didn't leave town. They didn't even know what lay beyond Wilder's three blocks of crumbling whitewashed buildings: a taqueria, a hardware store, a barbershop, a post office. Boise, forty-five minutes to the east, was far. It was bright lights, big city. Boise was the shit, and every day they asked, "Miss Lopedi, did you come from Boise today?"

"I did," I'd say.

"You live in Boise?"

"I do."

"You married, Miss Lopedi?"

"No."

"You're too pretty to not be married," they would say. "How old are you?"

"That's a secret."

I'd given them my age before, but they always forgot, which was a good thing. To them I could have been sixteen or forty, and it wouldn't have mattered. I was older, and older was old enough to be married.

"Miss Lopedi, do you have a house in the Boise city?"

"I have an apartment, and a cat who lives with me."

"That's cool," they'd say. "That is so cool. We want to visit you in Boise someday."

THE PHONE RANG. When Val answered his voice went suddenly high and soft, and I knew it was a woman. I felt like a big wind entered me. He cradled the cordless between his neck and shoulder and walked into the basement. I shuffled to the edge of the stairs. He laughed as if he and whoever was on the other end were old friends, and my head felt light with anger, and I shook, like my arms and legs were wires, a pulse of electric cords gone haywire.

I opened up his refrigerator. There was a jar of mayonnaise, a jar of dill pickles, a pitcher of pink guava drink he made from a frozen can, two eggs, and a block of molding Gouda. He had half a bottle of Absolut in the freezer.

"Don't mind if I do," I said, and pointed my glass toward the floor, toward him in the basement. "This is a great party. Do I want to dance? I'd love to dance," I said to the refrigerator. I turned on some music, this time A-ha, but instead I leaned against the wall and sipped vodka. I felt sad and old. I felt I'd missed something along the way, necessary information on dating that my friends seemed to know: when to stay, when to leave, how to get what you wanted, how to get your man to commit. I was honest and naively hopeful about love, yet there I was dating a thirty-eight-year-old man with secrets and lies. A man in his basement talking to another woman on the phone while I stood in my stupid outfit in his kitchen, waiting for him to choose me.

I edged down the steep, dark stairs. He held the phone away from his face, his palm clamped over the receiver. "What?" He brushed his hand in the air for me to leave, and retreated further into the laundry room.

I wasn't a desperate woman. I wanted my life to be noticed by someone, I wanted a witness, I wanted to be a witness. It was simple—I wanted love. I wanted to thread my life with another's and make something for ourselves. Love is no small thing.

* * *

I SMOKED CIGARETTES in the backyard. It was a clear, cold night, and the stars were shiny blue dots hanging above me. Our carved pumpkins glowed and flickered by the back door. My pumpkin had long, slender curved cuts like peony petals falling all over, and Val's was a work of art—he was a painter, and had special blades and X-ACTO knives and knew how to use them. He'd carved the head of a dragon, and its body and tail swept around the orange globe. With the candle lit, the dragon looked like it was swimming in the dark. The doorbell rang, kids coming for candy, but I stayed outside, my silly white dress reflecting the candlelight like a big moon.

The winter before, the elk came down into the valley for food, down from the mountains and sharp rock ridgelines and canyon cliffs. They came down every year and always made a safe trip, but last year was different. They walked out onto the reservoir where the ice wasn't thick enough to hold them, fell through, and kept coming and falling into the water and dying. They froze, and the ice froze back up around them. Their bodies were half-submerged, and from a distance they looked like seals lying curled on a beach. Their antlers were above the ice, sticking out like tree branches.

The Forest Service tried to block them. They set up alternate routes, but it didn't take. They tried to scare them away, and that didn't work either. What drew them to the reservoir? The elk were dying and stuck, and we all wondered what would happen come spring, come the quick thaw from a strong sun in late February. I imagined swimming in summer, elk lying at the bottom of the reservoir under the dark of the cool water, like giant sleeping fish. I imagined them still there, bodies turning into bones in the quiet, the cold coming back and the water getting ready for another freeze—the ice like a lid, keeping the world and the sun from reaching them. I hoped the elk knew better this year. I hoped they'd take a different path.

VAL'S FOOTSTEPS CAME UP the basement stairs. A block of light entered the yard as the door opened and he peeked out.

"Who is she?" I asked.

He took small, slow steps like a tiptoe toward me, then stood and looked up at the sky with his hands in his pockets. "I met her last night. I didn't expect she'd call."

"What the fuck is your problem?"

"I don't have a problem. I can do whatever I want."

"You know, Val, I think I saw your face in one of the carved pumpkins smashed alongside the road earlier."

There was a party at the house behind us, across the alley, where women threw fire. They tossed and waved batons of flames in the air. They danced around in shiny black flapper dresses to music that sounded like it was being broadcast over a loudspeaker from Morocco—flutes and drums and brass instruments that sounded hot, dusty, and exotic—music that charmed snakes and animals in trees and brought birds down from the sky. Their yard was packed with friends looking on while drinking beers, some shoulders touching for the first time, others long in love. You could always tell.

A car screeched and revved through the alley. The driver wore a rainbow wig and a red clown nose, and beeped and waved as he passed.

"A tragicomedy, this is," I said aloud, to no one in particular. "A sad sad string of foolish events."

"Don't be so dramatic, Jenni. You're so goddamn serious about everything."

The phone rang again. The cordless was in the basement. I moved to stand in the doorway. He stood in front of me. The pumpkins' light flickered against the grass and the side of the house.

"This is serious," I said.

"Move," he said. "You're in my way." He raised his hand, and I flinched. He wiped his mouth on his wristband.

"Don't say that," I said. "Don't ever say that again. What are you doing?"

He folded his lips in tight and shook his head back and forth. "I'm going out. I'm getting out of here." He shoved past me into the house. I heard him clinking glasses in the kitchen, moving plates in the sink, then the front door slamming.

I stood in the backyard and waited for Val to return. I waited for him to explain all this, or tell me something, anything. I thought maybe he'd say, *I shouldn't have talked to her* or *I love you* or even *It's over for us, and I'm sorry. I'm so very sorry* or *I'm a liar and a sneak and I wish you'd figured out sooner.* I wanted any tiny explanation or apology.

I should have seen this coming, but I hadn't. I should have left him when he started playing poker games in secret basements until four in the morning, when he began falling into a debt he couldn't get out of and drinking more steadily than ever, but I was naïve. I'd never met someone like him before. I didn't know these things were problems until they'd already happened over and over again and I was already in love and in too deep. He was a man rocking on the precipice, which was exactly where he wanted to be. He loved his dark, secret life more than anything, more than he ever loved or would love me. I couldn't save him because he didn't want to be saved. He was exactly where he wanted to be.

I wasn't the kind of person to make a scene. I was a teacher. I had a reputation to watch. I had to be someone who could take care of fourth-graders. Someone who didn't drink by herself four nights a week, or drive around until three in the morning to see whether her boyfriend came home. Who does that? I did that. I'd lost my sense of normal.

Every day at school I thought that if these kids' parents knew who I was, what I did in my personal time, they wouldn't want their kid near me. But I was a pretty and pleasant young woman. I dressed well, was articulate, was gentle with the children. The kids got away with much more when I had a hangover. Some days they thought I had a cold and didn't feel well, and they hushed each other, acted like little adults, putting their index fingers over their lips and whispering, "Ms. Lopedi's not feeling good. Hush it up."

It was those days I wished for the kids never to know what I knew about how twisted and irrational love can make us, how sick we can make ourselves over love, or losing love. I hoped they wouldn't find themselves in a place like mine. It was strange how I could guess what kind of adults the children might become, guess at the decisions they'd make and the lives they'd lead. Julio would be a middle manager at Best Buy and wear cheap button-down shirts; Isobel would be a veterinarian; Brett would be a meth dealer. But there were always surprises. I never thought I'd end up being this kind of person. I don't think anyone did: mid-thirties, unmarried, childless, living in a small apartment, in debt and barely scraping by. Did my third-grade teacher, Mrs. Rubin, look at me all those years ago and think, *Jenni's going to be unlucky in love and date men who are unstable and unreliable, and she'll be a teacher wearing worn-out clothes.* Did she think, *Poor Jenni?*

PEOPLE CLAPPED AND WHISTLED in the fire-throwers' backyard. I walked through the alley and up to their fence. I didn't feel strange standing there watching, because it was a sight and everyone was watching. The batons traced circles of orange in the dark; they were beautiful serpents of light flying through the air. The women were young, their dresses sparkling, their faces shining. I used to be like those women. I wanted to be like them again. That night, I ached for youth. I didn't want to be young so much as have the feeling of hope and possibility in front of me again. I'd tucked it away someplace, and I couldn't remember where.

The yard glowed and looked as warm as a cozy living room. I wanted to step in, thaw out, be among the happy others. There were three women with fire, and the one in the middle, Starr was her name, looked my way. She looped a large circle of fire around the crown of her head, a halo, and winked.

I was freezing, and my fingers were numb. I went inside and held my hands under warm water in the kitchen sink to get some feeling back. All the lights were on, and I went through and turned them off. I locked the doors, went into Val's bedroom, and lay down. I turned on the bedside lamp, a kitchy vintage one with a small metal cylindrical shade—1950s, Val's favorite for clothes, furniture, everything. His room had a musty smell of things old and used, a smell that didn't come out with hot water and soap.

Val shopped at every Salvation Army, every Youth Ranch, and every secondhand store he could find. I loved old things and the search for treasures too, but I hated hunting with Val, because it was about his image, and his image was vintage and his image was antinew, anticorporate, antinormalcy, which included marriage, babies, owning a house or car or anything over thirty dollars, and perhaps having sex with one woman at a time. It would have been one thing if he were twenty and going through a phase, but he was a grown man still fighting for his image, still holding on to his cool, afraid to be known. What he saw as his freedom, I saw as him moving closer and closer toward the loneliest place in the world.

I opened his desk drawer. My heart beat fast and hard. *This is bad*, I told myself; *you shouldn't do this.* I touched things, delicately, making sure everything I picked up went back in its place. Matchbooks, pens, pencils, small scraps of paper with over twenty phone numbers: Bridget, Noel, Katy, Lisa, Annie, Amy, Mary, Angela. A list of names right in front of me of who he'd fucked or would fuck.

Right beside the bed he had a giant map of the United States on the wall, an old scroll-style school map with the states colored bright yellows, pinks, oranges, greens, and a pleasing bright blue for oceans and lakes. The R was missing from Harbor off the Gulf coast of Florida, and it read Harbo. I ran my foot over the thick paper and pointed my big toe at Idaho. "You are here," I said, and dragged my foot across the map to California. "But maybe you belong here in the sunshine." Then I slid my toe to Montana. "Or here you could work on a horse ranch, which you've always wanted to do." I slid my toe and circled it around New Hampshire, Vermont, and Massachusetts. "Or here you could be close to family and friends. People who know you. People who give a shit."

When I asked my mother for advice, which was often, she told me you could love someone, and love them fiercely, but that didn't mean you should carve out a life together. She said, "Jenni, just because you love someone doesn't mean he's good for you." And now I understood what she meant. Now I knew that love wasn't all you needed, love didn't conquer all, and that bad love could make you crazy and lonely and a lesser version of yourself. It could almost make you drown and never resurface. It could make you disappear.

I slid my big toe down toward Connecticut and New York and felt lonely and far away from everyone and everything that mattered, from people who knew a better, happier version of me. A me before I began circling in this stuck place, with a stuck man whose problems I couldn't fix and had no business trying to fix.

The doorbell rang. I walked through the dark house to the front door and peeked through the side window. Two kids stood on the stoop: one wore a sheet with cut-out eyeholes and the words *I am a ghost* written across his chest, and a girl wore a black leotard, cat-ear headband, and had black whiskers painted on her cheeks and a pink circle on her nose.

The ghost opened the screen door, and its hinges squeaked and creaked.

"No one's home," the girl said.

"Worth a try," he said and knocked three heavy knocks. "Their pumpkins are lit."

The girl moved toward the window where I stood in the dark, looking out at them. She looked in, right at my face. We were nose to nose. She looked into my eyes and her breath fogged up the glass, but she didn't *see* me. She was young, had so much to discover, and for a moment I remembered being that girl and imagining all the lives I might lead: adventure, romance, glamour, greatness, Paris, Vietnam, Wife, Mother. I had been excited to see who I'd become, but now all I had become was a woman waiting, afraid to ask for the things I wanted. The girl pressed her nose to the glass and backed away, proud of her print on the window. "Maybe they're asleep," she said, "but I've left my mark."

"I'm not asleep," I whispered, and then said more loudly, "I'm not asleep."

"Hello?" the boy said. "Did I hear someone in there?"

"Yes." I pushed my body up against the locked door with a thud. "But who am I? What am I? Hoooo ha ha ha ha!"

"I don't know," the boy said. The girl giggled, a high, rolling giggle like a twittering bird in a tree. "Why don't you open the door so we can find out? This ghost could use a Snickers or Mars bar."

A cheer rose from the backyard fire-throwing crowd— hooting, hollering, and clapping. Val didn't have any candy for trick-or-treaters, because Val was that kind of guy, the kind who didn't like to give anything away—a cheap, selfish, lying sonofabitch. What did it say about me that I'd loved him all this time, and what did that make me? Blind? Stupid? A woman willing to be treated badly for a scrap of affection? I walked back to Val's room, opened his drawer, and took the pieces of paper with the women's names and phone numbers.

"Come on," the boy said and knocked again. "We can't wait on this doorstep forever."

I slid the chain off its groove and unlocked the bolt with a click.

"Ooooh, I'm scared," the girl said.

The door sucked open. "Nothing to be scared of," I said, and flicked on the porch light. They squinted at the brightness. "No more waiting."

"Trick or treat," the boy said.

"Nice dress," the girl said. "What are you supposed to be?"

"I'm a prom queen," I said. "Listen, I ran out of candy, but I have something else for you." I held out the pieces of paper in my palms like offerings. "These are secret numbers. These women have special powers and hold the answers to the universe."

"Like witches?" the girl asked.

"Something like that."

"Cool," the boy said. "Like psychics or seers. I'll take one."

"You can have them all," I said. They opened up their pillowcases and waited. I held the pieces of paper above each case and let them fall like feathers—the weightless names of strange women drifting into their lives, women they might call and ask about the galaxy or their parents' divorce or geometry or if their crush will ask them to the winter formal. Women who might hang up on them, or who might give the answer they've been looking for all their young lives. You never know what will happen. That's the strangeness of life. You can't know what, when, how, or why any one thing will happen. You can't predict a thing.

"Thanks, lady," the ghost said.

"Go find the answers to the universe for me," I said.

They walked down the sidewalk to the house next door, and I stepped out into the night and shut the door behind me. I bent down and lifted the tops off the pumpkins and blew out the candles. I picked up the smaller pumpkin first and threw it at the side of the stucco house. It smashed into bits, and stringy orange pumpkin insides stuck to the white wall. The kids turned and watched me from next door; Old Man Dan, the neighbor, poked his head out and waved. He wore a Frankenstein mask. I picked up the bigger pumpkin and placed it in the middle of the porch. I stood on top of it until it caved in, and then I stomped and kicked until it was flat and broken.

"I think the prom queen's crazy," the cat girl said.

"That's Jenni; she's a nice girl. Hey, Jenni, you're a nice girl, aren't you?" Old Man Dan yelled over, his voice muffled under his mask.

"I'm the best girl," I said. "I'm the best girl this two-bit piece of shit will ever meet, and he never even knew it."

The pumpkin lay splayed on the cement. I dug my heels into its heart and fucked up the slimy center until it looked like something else entirely, something unrecognizable, and something I could walk away from.

THE GENIUS OF LOVE

WE WERE ALL NERVOUS for my sister, Elena, to come home. It was April, I was finishing high school in Vermont, and Elena was being sent home early from an outdoor program for delinquent kids in California: she'd accidentally cut her thumb off, right above the knuckle, trying to split firewood with a hatchet. She had been gone three weeks, and the house had been quiet, a nice quiet, and I think it scared us that we got used to her being gone and it being OK. But my father was still mad. A silent sort of mad where he walked out of rooms and banged things around, and sometimes left without saying where he was going.

The headmaster from Danville Day School had called at the end of March to say rumors had spread and that someone had caught Elena and Mr. Rich kissing in a janitorial closet. Elena was a sophomore and taking Italian from Mr. Rich, Massimo Rich, last name originally Richaroni, who was twenty-four and couldn't keep his hands off her. Not to blame it all on Mr. Rich, because Elena wasn't the whitest angel on the block, as my father had said before. But Mr. Rich was eight years older, and engaged to Ms. Krick, the Latin teacher, and had no right putting his hands on Elena.

The headmaster said Mr. Rich was fired, then thanked my parents for their support and steady donations to the school, praised Elena's performance on the field hockey team, told them I was a shoo-in for the University of Vermont, and asked if my parents wanted to press charges. My father kept saying, "I don't know. What do you do in these situations? I have no idea. Mr. Rich seemed perfectly nice, so this is all very hard to believe." When he got off the phone he said, "They were caught in a janitor's closet. Do you know what they keep in those closets?" My mother and I looked at him but didn't say anything. "Bleach, dirty mops and buckets, aerosol spray cans—things you don't want to touch or inhale."

My mother had a box of tissues in front of her, her nose red and chapped from blowing it and crying, and she put her hand on my back. "Did you know about this, Cate? Did you hear the rumors?"

"No," I said, and I hadn't, not of an affair. I had seen Elena and Mr. Rich talking a lot, but that was the kind of school we went to—a small tight-knit place where teachers were advisors and coaches, people who cared. I heard people saying they thought Mr. Rich and Elena flirted, but that didn't surprise me. A lot of people flirted with Elena, and she was good at flirting back. She was one of those girls everyone liked being near.

"We've met this man," my father said, and rubbed his head near the base of his neck where he still had hair, "last year at the fall picnic. Do you think he had his dirty paws all over Elena then?"

"I hope not," my mother said. She wet a tissue with her tongue and ran it under her eye to wipe away smudged mascara.

"What do we do? Do we put a twenty-four-year-old in jail? Or should we be satisfied that he's not at Danville Day anymore, and get on with our lives?"

"We've got to do something," my mother said, and threw her tissue hard at my father, but it landed, covered with black mascara spots, on the middle of the kitchen table.

My mother picked Elena up at school, and that night my father couldn't look at her. My mother spent hours in Elena's room, talking in hushed tones. One week later she was on a plane to California. The school counselor recommended the outdoor program; she said it was a place where kids survived with the bare necessities, and were forced to take a good look at what they were doing and why.

THE SNOW HAD MELTED, and the air warmed and felt soft the weeks Elena was gone. I was accepted into the University of Vermont. My mother bought books on teenage girls and talked about ways we could help Elena when she came home. My mother used the phrases "inner strength," "confidence building," and "moral support." My father twisted his hands, and only once I heard him say, *That sick sonofabitch.* I knew Mr. Rich was too old, and Elena too young. I knew what happened was wrong, but I wondered if maybe Elena and Mr. Rich really did care about each other and if that mattered at all.

I'd always been careful. I drank, but never got caught. I sneaked out and lied about parties, but I hadn't done things Elena had done—smoked pot, had sex, or taken the car and left the house even after our parents told her she couldn't. Elena seemed dangerous to me, but there was something brave in all that she did. She did what she wanted. There were times I wondered why I hadn't done those things, made up my own mind, taken that goddamn car and left when I felt like it.

MY PARENTS LEFT for Logan Airport at five on a rainy Friday evening. Elena's flight came in late, so they were spending the night at a hotel in Boston. Our house was quiet and water beaded on the windows. I stood at the front door, leaned my forehead into the screen, and smelled the metal, the rain, the mud. Outside, the grass had started to green and the maples and dogwoods to bud, and I hoped spring would come early, warm things up and get them blooming, because then maybe we'd all feel good, and be all right.

I went upstairs to Elena's room. My mother had cleaned it up. Clothes were folded and neatly hung, the bed was perfectly made, and nothing was on the floor. I stood in front of her dresser, picked up her perfumes and smelled them: Two were sweet and watery, and two were soft and spicy. I looked at myself in her mirror. I pulled up my hair, which was straight and long, and held it on top of my head.

Elena knew things, and I wondered how she came to know them. I was sure she had left to learn something I never would—something you could only learn from having older lovers, or from sleeping in the desert in the middle of nowhere. It seemed so strange to me how different we were. How had that happened when we seemed to share the same life, in the same house, sleeping in rooms next to each other our whole lives?

We didn't look alike. Elena was tall, blond, and full-figured. She wore leather, boots with heels, choker necklaces, and eyeshadow. I was shorter, a brunette, and wore clothes that didn't get in the way of moving around. Elena smoked cigarettes and said she knew the world. Said she knew what was real out there and that she was sick and tired of being stuck in a farm-fuck town in Vermont. She said she knew she belonged somewhere bigger like New York, Paris, or Venice. "Bye-bye, au revoir, ciao," she had started saying on the phone to her friends, and to us as she left the house weekend nights.

I ATE LEFTOVER CHICKEN and poured a glass of white wine from an open bottle in the refrigerator. I took the wine upstairs and stood in front of the bathroom mirror. When I set the glass down on the counter it made a nice clinking noise, so I picked it up and did it again. I tried to imagine what Elena's thumb would look like with half of it gone. Something short and stubby. Something you see other people missing and guess they were born that way. I had a deep scar from the thorn of a rosebush that scratched the length of my arm. People would look at it, and I told them it was from a mountain lion attack in Colorado. Sometimes they believed me. I was glad Elena had her own story to tell, and I thought to tell her scars could make you tough, give you a history right on your own body.

I took off my shirt to search my arm. The scar was a faint line, almost gone. In the mirror, my hair looked thinned out and scraggly. I spread a towel on the floor beneath me. I brushed my hair back into a low ponytail at the base of my neck and took scissors from under the sink. I held onto the loose hair and cut right under the elastic, then tied the elastic around the cut hair. It looked like a thick brown piece of rope.

My hair was short and crooked above my shoulders and brushed against my neck. My head felt lighter, and I felt good. I put my cut hair into an envelope and wrote on a piece of paper—*April 18th. Elena comes home tomorrow from the desert. My hair, eighteen years old. From now on I will be more brave. In college, I would like to fall in love.* I put the paper in with my hair and sealed the envelope. I put it in the plastic box where I kept other envelopes I'd made for times I wanted to remember, for times I'd made promises to myself. I had photographs, handmade jewelry, my ex-boyfriend's eyelash, my best friend's blood on a piece of paper. I had foreign money, sand from Hawaii, a dried cornstalk from Ohio where my grandfather was buried, and a small, smooth rock from the river where I had my first kiss.

I went into Elena's room and put on a pair of her high heels and a black sequined dress she wore to last year's prom. I put on mascara, gray sparkly eyeshadow, and red lipstick. I took a cigarette from Elena's desk and walked downstairs to turn out lights and pour more wine. I stood on the front porch and smoked. It was dark. Our house was secluded—out front a large lawn and a quarter-mile-long dirt driveway that led to a country road, behind us a field and an apple orchard. I always asked questions as a kid that my parents couldn't answer—how asphalt got its name, about time travel, and what it would be like to die. There, that night, I wondered who we were, my family, and where we were going. I wondered if there was any way to know. I felt for the first time that my life was about to become of my own making, of my own decisions and choice. It made my heart beat faster.

I wanted to ask Mr. Rich if he loved Elena, and I wanted to know why. But I didn't want to call and have him think it was a prank. His house was in the center of town—a small white clapboard colonial with a red door and a porch. I put on my long winter coat and drove there.

I PARKED BEHIND the Town Hall. There was a creepy old cemetery with thin, leaning headstones of the first people who lived here. Mr. Rich lived a block away. I walked slowly in the heels. My ankles wobbled, and I stepped carefully, heel, toe, heel, toe. Houses butted right up to the road. Some had carriage posts from the olden days, and some had white picket fences. Houses were lit from within, warm light spilling out into the night. The sequins on Elena's prom dress sparkled dully, like stars coming through clouds.

It wasn't late, only nine. Mr. Rich's green Saab was parked on the street. The house across from his was dark, so I stood on their lawn behind a tree. His lights were on, and I could see in. Tall wooden bookcases lined his living room. An old poster of a beautiful woman in a long purple gown with a martini in her hand, and something written in Italian underneath, was framed on the wall. His window was open a little, and I heard piano and flute music. The rain had stopped, the ground was wet and soggy, and cool air seeped up under my coat and over my legs.

Before Elena left, I asked her what Mr. Rich was like. "He knows what he wants," she said, and I wondered if she meant he knew he wanted to live in Vermont, teach Italian, and wear tweed jackets, or if he knew he wanted to have sex with her. Elena only had one boyfriend before, Tommy Burton, in the eighth grade. She lost her virginity to him in his parents' barn on wood plank boards, and came home with splinters in her back. Now there was Mr. Rich and janitorial closets, and I wanted to tell her she was better than that.

I stepped out from behind the tree to cross the street. It was a small, old road with nothing between his house and me. My heels clicked on the cracked and uneven pavement as I slowly walked the fifty feet. I took deliberate steps toward the blooming yellow daffodils in front of the porch rail from where I could peek into their windows. I was close; I made it onto the lawn where my heels sunk into wet ground, when a chair pushed back on the porch, and Mr. Rich stood shadowed against the light of his window.

"Mrs. Whitaker?" he asked. "Is that you?"

I froze.

"Is everything all right?" he asked.

My instinct was to run, but my body felt heavy, my legs stiff. I couldn't run in the heels anyway, and I didn't want to be afraid of Mr. Rich. I moved out from the shadows and stood in front of his porch light.

"Cate Mahoney?" Mr. Rich asked. "What are you doing?"

"I was curious."

Mr. Rich walked down the stairs and stood in front of me on his lawn. He held a glass with clear liquor in it.

"Do your parents know you're here?" He leaned in and bent his head down to look me in the eyes. His breath had a strong licorice smell, and his hair was messy, as if he'd been running his hands through it.

"I just wanted to see"—I looked past him, into his house—"what you're like."

He stood up, shifted his weight, and raised his arms at his sides. "Nothing much to see," he said quietly, and took a sip of his drink. He leaned back against the railing. It was shiny, white paint, not a chip anywhere.

"What's the poster say?"

He turned to read it. "*Intelletto d'amore*," he said, smiling.

"What's that mean?"

"The genius of love." He faced me and seemed pleased. A car passed by. Mr. Rich's eyes shone for a moment in the headlights and went dark again.

Then a woman's voice came from inside, and said, "Who are you talking to?" and I knew it was Ms. Krick. I took Latin for three years.

Mr. Rich put his arm out to touch my shoulder, but I backed away.

"Do you need a ride home?" he asked.

"Why is she here?"

He bit his lip and gave me this look like he was really sorry. Then he folded his arms and sighed. "It's all very complicated," he said. "Maybe one day you'll understand."

Ms. Krick came to the window. She wore a bathrobe and pulled it tight around her waist. She looked out at us with squinted eyes as if we were far away. I don't think she knew it was me with the short hair and all the makeup on.

"Don't you love Elena?" I whispered.

Mr. Rich looked over his shoulder at Ms. Krick, then back at me and closed his eyes. "I don't know what to say," he said.

AT NOON THE NEXT DAY my father's car pulled up in our circular driveway. I stood on the porch steps. My father strode toward me, and my mother and sister barely had their doors open when he said, "What did she do the first thing at the hotel? She called that goddamn Italian and talked for twenty minutes. She called from a pay phone in the lobby, thinking we wouldn't know she was missing and come looking for her." He walked past me into the house.

I watched as my mother and sister took bags from the trunk. Elena had a cast on that covered her left thumb and wrist. When she got close, I went up to her. She didn't hug me, just leaned into me, and I put my arms around her and squeezed. "Welcome back to our happy home," I said.

"Right," she said, and went straight upstairs. I started up after her, but my mother touched me at my elbow and said, "I think you should leave her alone. What did you do to your hair?" I shrugged, and went to Elena's room anyway. Her door was cracked, and I knocked lightly and walked in.

"What do you want?" she said, her back to me.

She unpacked her clothes with one hand: four pairs of underpants, two T-shirts, two pairs of socks, one wool sweater, one raincoat, a pair of hiking boots, a toothbrush, and a pair of canvas pants my mother bought for her at the Farm-Way store.

"Can you believe this?" she said. "I was smelly for three weeks and learned how to build a fire with a stick and then cut half my arm off."

"Your thumb," I said.

"A thumb is as good as an arm."

"Does it hurt?"

"Everything hurts."

She walked to her desk, opened the bottom drawer, lifted piles of papers, and took out a pack of cigarettes. She hoisted up the window and knelt on the floor. Then she popped open the corner of the screen and lit her cigarette.

"Did Mr. Rich say anything when you called him?"

"Sure," she said, and put her lips to the screen and blew out smoke. "He said all sorts of things." She had tears in her eyes. "I'm not playing a game," she said. "This isn't a game."

I sat next to her and put my arm around her shoulder. She was very warm, as if she'd just been in the sun, or was sick and overheated. She didn't wear any makeup, and looked more herself— clear white skin, and eyebrows so blond they were hardly there. She flicked her cigarette out into the air and took my hand in her good hand, and I wondered if my parents had even touched her like this yet, and knew they probably hadn't for fear of Elena thinking all was forgotten and forgiven.

"They just don't want to look bad. This is about them looking bad." Then she wiped her nose on her sleeve and looked around her room. "Would you just leave me alone?" She sat there with her cast in her lap, running her fingers over it as if she could feel something underneath.

AT NINE THAT NIGHT my mother, father, and I were in the family room watching a war movie about Vietnam. My mother and father sat on the couch, and I was in a chair on the other side of the room, wrapped up in a blanket. None of us had said a thing about Elena all day, but then she came down from her room and stood in front of us.

"My love for Mr. Rich is real," she said.

I hadn't told anyone about the night before, about Ms. Krick in her bathrobe. My father's face went red, and veins came up high on his forehead. I thought for sure one would pop, and that would be it. He said, "It's for real, huh? What exactly does real mean when you're sixteen?"

Elena stood in front of us. She had something to tell my parents, had probably been in her room that whole time thinking about telling them, maybe even writing it down to get it right. Her cast looked thick and heavy, and had writing all over it in black and red pen—people's names, and things like, "Way to go," "Ciao," "Good luck," and "We'll miss you."

"I'm not a baby, Dad," Elena said. "I can fall in love."

"That's what you think," my father said, and kept his eyes on the screen, on a scene where a helicopter got shot, tilted to one side in the air, then hit a tree and blew up. I had the remote and turned off the television, but my father didn't shift his gaze.

"What about his fiancée, Ms. Krick? Did you think of how you hurt her?" my father said. "He could go to jail—what do you think about that?" My father crossed his legs, and his slipper slid off his foot as his leg came down, but he didn't do anything about it, and sat there with a bare foot.

"No one's going to jail," my mother said, and leaned forward. She had on her nightgown, and her long legs stuck out from under it. She ran her hands up and down the length of her calves, how you would rub someone's back while telling them things would be all right.

"Why can't you accept that I love Massimo?" Elena said.

"Massimo," my father said. "What the hell kind of name is that anyway?" And he clapped his hands together.

"Elena, we just want to understand what's going on," my mother said.

"What are you trying to do?" my father said. "Make us crazy?"

"Fuck it," Elena said. "I'm trying to tell you something, but fuck it all."

"OK," my father said. "Just fuck it all."

Elena spun away, and her footsteps were heavy and loud on the stairs. My parents weren't going to listen to Elena, weren't going to hear a thing. I thought they owed her that much, at least that.

My father stood. He lowered his head to his chest and kept it there. Then he let out a breath and walked upstairs with one slipper on, leaving the other where it fell on the rug.

My mother stood. "This isn't love. I hope you see that, Cate." She picked up my father's slipper and walked out. I heard her get a glass of water in the kitchen, and then she said, "Goodnight," almost to herself, but loud enough for me to hear.

The refrigerator clicked and hummed in the kitchen, and I heard my parents' voices in their room above me through the grate in the ceiling. I thought of standing on the fireplace hearth, to get closer to listen, but I didn't want to hear their reasons for why they believed it wasn't love.

I turned on the television. The war movie was over, replaced by a classic with people kissing in a close-up shot. They kissed a closed-mouth kiss, and I wondered why we were all so afraid, all of us except Elena, of falling in love with the wrong people or doing something we weren't supposed to do. Whether Mr. Rich loved Elena or not didn't seem to matter then. I wasn't sure if he did, having Ms. Krick in his house in her bathrobe. But Elena loved him, and I thought it so brave. She felt something and didn't make excuses.

THE NEXT MORNING I woke up late and went downstairs. No one was around, so I walked into the garage to see what cars were there. As I got to the door, I heard my father saying, "Fuck, fuck, fuck." He didn't hit or throw anything. He didn't yell. He just stood in the corner by the shelf that held softball mitts, ski boots, plastic tarps, and turpentine bobbing his head up and down as he spoke. A patch of light came through the window and landed on his right shoulder. It was a yellow morning-in-spring light. Then he turned and saw me. He sat down in my great-grandmother's old oak rocking chair, next to a cardboard box and a stack of newspapers. I walked over and put my hand on his shoulder.

"I'm OK," he said, and looked around the garage. He cupped his hand over his mouth and shook his head.

I thought I'd stay with him a while longer. It was something I thought I should do. He was my father. I wanted him to know none of it was about him. I wanted him to know daughters loved their fathers, but fell in love, even as teenagers, sometimes with the wrong people for brief amounts of time.

"Nothing will come of it," I said.

He nodded. Then he picked up my hand and held it. "I like you with shorter hair," he said. "You look like a college student."

MY FATHER INVITED Mr. Rich over for dinner. I was in the room when he called and told him to come over at seven, and that we'd be eating American food—steaks, green beans, and salad, and drinking a nice bottle of red from California. I thought there was no way he'd say yes, but then my father said, "OK? OK. Be here at seven." He hung up, and said he was going to the store to buy food.

"It's not a good idea," I said.

"He's coming for dinner. It's about time." He smiled and gathered his wallet and keys. "It will be fine, Cate."

24

"Are you sure?"

"I don't know what else to do," he said.

WHEN MY MOTHER and sister came home at five, my father and I sat in the family room reading the newspaper. He read about politics and stocks; I read about fashion and travel. When they walked in, my father said, "Mr. Rich is coming for dinner at seven."

"What?" Elena said. I noticed her cast was off, but I couldn't see her thumb.

"Oh, good Christ," my mother said.

Elena flung her shopping bags on the floor and said, "What's wrong with you? Are you sick?"

My father folded his paper on his lap. "I thought if you're in love with this young man, I want to get a look at the two of you together."

"Oh, for real, Dad."

"For real, Elena. I want to see this Massimo up close with my daughter. We're having steak, beans, and salad."

"Was this the best thing to do?" My mother said.

"I don't know," my father said.

"You did this," my mother said. "Just remember when seven comes around that you set this up. It's your dinner, you're cooking." She picked up Elena's bags and walked upstairs.

WHEN THE DOORBELL RANG, I half-expected Ms. Krick to be with Mr. Rich. My father had already drunk half a bottle of Cakebread Cellars cabernet, his special wine, and his cheeks were red.

"You'd better get that," my father said to my mother. "I'll be out at the grill."

My mother turned down the front hall. Elena and I stood in the kitchen next to one another. Elena looked nervous, even scared, like she regretted getting herself into all this in the first place. She was very still, and touched the scar that looked like a piece of shiny red wax rounded over where the top of her thumb should have been.

"You're OK," I said, looking at her.

"I don't think so," she said, and tears welled in her eyes. "This isn't OK."

My mother opened the door, said hello in a high-pitched way that made me know it was fake and strained, and shook Mr. Rich's hand.

"Come in," she said, one hand extended toward Elena and me, and with the other shut the door behind him. He wore an ironed, buttoned shirt, a tweed jacket, and khakis. He looked nice, and walked in behind my mother. He held a bottle of wine in front of him, a shield of sorts—something to keep between us.

"Hi, girls," he said, and smiled at us as if he were my parents' friend and not my sister's lover. I waved at him, even though he was close.

"Massimo," Elena said, "you didn't have to do this."

Mr. Rich set the bottle of wine on the island and put his hands on Elena's shoulders, as if to straighten them out. Then he took her hand, the one with the bad thumb, and kissed it. My mother pretended not to watch, and made noise near the sink with plates.

"It's so ugly," Elena said.

Mr. Rich said something in Italian that I didn't understand, and he kissed Elena's thumb again. I was surprised he kissed her, that he did it in front of us, and that he did it after I saw him two nights before with Ms. Krick.

Then my father walked in with his grill mitts on and a long poker fork in his hand.

"Massimo," he said. "I'm glad you're here. I'm glad we can get to know each other."

"OK, Mr. Mahoney. Me too, then."

"Call me Tom," my father said. He picked up the bottle of wine Mr. Rich brought and clinked the poker fork against it. "What's this here?"

"Some Italian wine, something I thought we could drink with your American dinner," Mr. Rich said.

My mother gave my father a look. We all gave him a look.

"Good," my father said. "That'll be fine."

My mother opened cabinets and took out wineglasses. "Why don't we all sit at the table," she said, "and talk?"

Mr. Rich sat next to Elena, and I sat across from them. My father eyed him while he opened a second bottle of Cakebread cabernet. He poured three glasses and handed one to Mr. Rich.

"We'll start with this," my father said. "You are old enough to drink, right?"

Mr. Rich gave a tight, fake smile. "I think we all know my age here."

"I think you're right," my father said.

My mother, at the stove, said, "Aren't you brought up drinking wine in Italy?"

"In most families children are served a little wine with dinner."

"Not in this part of the world," my father said. "Things are different here."

"They are very different," Mr. Rich said.

"Now," my father hesitated, and pulled at his eyebrow, "do all Italians date sixteen-year-old girls?" Elena was red, and looked as though she might jump out of her seat and punch our father in the face.

"Tom, don't," my mother said, holding a boiling pot of beans over the sink.

"Don't what?" my father said.

"He can say what he wants," Mr. Rich said.

"Dad, if you do this, I swear," Elena said. "I swear you won't see me for a long time."

Usually when Elena said those things, my father would go on, and dismiss her threat. But something stopped him. Maybe it was having Mr. Rich there, and my father saw that Elena could leave with him and be all right. My father picked up his grill mitts and poker fork and walked back outside, the screen door slapping shut behind him.

"This isn't easy," my mother said, looking at Mr. Rich.

"I apologize," Mr. Rich said. "It's not easy for me either, Mrs. Mahoney."

My mother paused. Then she poured the pot of beans and boiling water into a strainer in the sink. Steam lifted and fogged the window.

My father came back in with a platter of steaks. He put them on plates, then sat down next to me and across from Elena and Mr. Rich. My mother handed me a platter of green beans and sat at the end of the table next to Elena.

"Let's try this again," my father said, and lit a match and leaned in to light the candles in the middle of the table. "Why don't you tell me, Massimo, about what you're going to do now, and what your intentions are with my daughter?" He blew out the match, sat back in his chair, and crossed his arms. Mr. Rich sipped his wine and set the glass down carefully.

"I love your daughter very much," he said, and looked at Elena. She smiled at him and shook her head. Her eyes teared up, and I felt my own face turn red and something catch in my throat. I couldn't look at my parents. No one moved.

Mr. Rich laid his hands flat on the table and sat upright. "But Ms. Krick and I have decided to get married."

My mother gasped. My father rested his elbows on the table, shut his eyes, and rubbed his temples. He just rubbed and rubbed, like all of a sudden Elena not marrying Mr. Rich was a problem.

"There it is," Elena said softly.

"Did you know this?" my mother said to her.

"Yes," she whispered. She took a deep breath, and my mother reached over and put her hand on Elena's.

"Wait," my father said. "Wait just a minute." He stood and held himself by the edge of the table. He picked up the poker fork and held it inches under Mr. Rich's chin. "You make my daughter fall in love with you and then marry someone else weeks after you're caught kissing her in a filthy closet? I don't think so."

"Now, hold on," Mr. Rich said. "I didn't make Elena do anything."

"Like hell you didn't," my father leaned closer. The candles flickered, and my father's eyes were wide and wild. Mr. Rich sat still, looked right at him and waited, as though he deserved this or worse. But I saw Mr. Rich's fear: his nostrils flared, his jaw tensed, his hands flat on the table and ready to rise.

"Stop it, Tom," my mother said. "You've had too much to drink."

"I don't know what to do with you," my father said, "for breaking my daughter's heart." Mr. Rich closed his eyes, and his chest rose and fell as if he were holding back something inside himself from spilling out. I knew Mr. Rich wouldn't hurt my father. It wasn't anger he held back. I thought it was love, and a great sadness at the thought of breaking Elena's heart.

Elena stood and walked over to my father. He still leaned over the table, and she hugged him from the side, her face buried in his shirt behind his arm. "Dad," Elena said. Elena whispered something in his ear, and he seemed to collapse a little into her, then held her tight. He held her like I'd never seen him hold onto anyone.

Mr. Rich stood, and Elena slowly pulled away from my father. "Stay a little longer," she said to him. My father kissed Elena on the top of the head, smoothed her hair, and nodded OK.

We sat on the screened-in porch. My mother lit candles in glass hurricane vases, and a warm breeze blew over us. The air smelled dewy—an earthy, heady smell of things getting green, of life pushing up from the ground toward the sky, ready to burst into blossom. Mr. Rich reached into his tweed jacket and brought out a long, thin-necked glass bottle that had a cork in the top. He offered us grappa, and my parents thought it would be nice.

"Let the girls have a taste too?" Mr. Rich said, and looked at my father.

"Why not?" my father said.

Then Mr. Rich put his hand on top of Elena's, and I thought that was something, and I knew Mr. Rich was sorry he was leaving her.

My mother set down five squat, round glasses, and Mr. Rich poured from the delicate neck of the bottle and handed one to each of us. The grappa smelled strong and dry like rubbing alcohol, but with a hint of pear or raspberry.

"Grrrrappa," my father said, trying to roll his *R*'s.

"To your health," Mr. Rich said, and held his glass in the air.

"To good things," my father said, his glass in the air too.

Elena held her glass with both hands, and I saw her thumb, red and scarred—something she'd have her whole life—and I wondered if she'd always think of Mr. Rich when she touched it, or when she got older and another man would kiss it and tell her things would be all right. I wondered if later she'd think of Mr. Rich and regret any of it, and at that moment, I didn't think she would.

"And bella bella Elena," Mr. Rich said.

"Bella bella," my mother said slowly.

"Bella," my father said.

We all raised our glasses and clinked them over the candles on the table. The grappa was strong and hot in my mouth and in my throat all the way down. I felt it all the way into my stomach, but it felt good, as if it evaporated all that had been there before, and was making room for something new.

I stood and walked to the edge of the porch. I looked through the screen over the back lawn and the field behind it. There was a little light left at the far edge of the sky, a deep-blue twilight, where in some part of the world day had not yet ended. But directly in front of me was dark and shadow. I heard a small thud on the soft ground in the distance, the sound of something heavy dropping to stillness. I tried to focus my eyes. I swore there was a figure in the dark behind the woodpile. I thought it might have been Ms. Krick, come to look in on our lives. I wondered if I stepped away and were behind that woodpile, a stranger spying in, if this family and life would be something I'd envy or want.

I imagined Ms. Krick standing alone in the dark, waiting to hear or see something to help her understand Mr. Rich, this man she was going to take to have and to hold. I imagined her leaning into the rough and splintered wood, desperately waiting for something to explain how a girl almost half her age could occupy a part of him and own a space in his heart. I raised my hand and pressed it against the screen, and I kept it there. Because I knew someone was out there, wanting to be acknowledged, and waiting for a sign.

THESE THINGS HAPPEN

GEORGE WAS SIXTY, and one month retired. He'd been a lawyer for thirty-five years. Every Monday he came to Hal's on Main Street in his small New Hampshire town. There were chips in the coffee cups, but it was the best breakfast around, and the diner always smelled like butter and bacon. He sat in the booth by the window and looked out over the river that ran under an abandoned mill. Maple colors were bright against a flat steel-gray sky. He felt restless, as if he were young again and looking for his life. His wife, Christine, had told him to make a list of things he wanted to do. He took out a notepad and wrote—learn guitar, build a pine table and chairs, plant a garden in spring. There was a rapping on the window. It was Frank Farinella. George didn't know Frank well, but well enough to know he didn't like him. Frank saluted George. Then he mimed eating food off a fork and closed his eyes and smiled like he was in heaven.

George stayed very still and read his newspaper. He heard the diner door open and the little metal bell clink above it. Next thing he knew, Frank was standing at his booth, arm extended.

"Georgie," Frank said.

George stood. Frank had a hard, quick handshake. "Frank Farinella, how are things?"

Frank wore a sweater with their golf club logo on it—a pine tree with the name Eastman running through it in script. It was a mystery what Frank did for a living. He had a suspicious air about him. George liked to think he was in the Mob. Or maybe the witness protection program had brought him to this rural New England town where he'd been hiding out, playing golf.

"You know, you can call me Farinella—that's what my friends call me," Frank said and waited for George to call him Farinella.

"OK," George paused. "Farinella, how are things?"

"That's it," Frank said and clucked his tongue. "Things are things. How about you?"

"Things are things," George said, picking up his newspaper and waving it back and forth, as if that explained how things were. "You know." He hoped Frank would go away.

"Well," George said, but Frank held his hand in the air to stop him.

"Hold tight, Georgie," Frank said and walked to the counter, squeezing between people. Frank's trousers seemed too big, hiked up high on his waist and pulled tight with a belt. "Miss," Frank said loudly to the waitress, a heavy woman with black hair and tight blue jeans. She looked up from behind the counter, and Frank held onto his waistband. "Miss, send poached eggs and bacon to this booth here, where I'll be joining my friend." Frank pointed at George.

"Sure," she said.

"I'll take a coffee while I'm up here," Frank said. "And four quarters." He slapped a dollar bill on the counter, and she handed him a mug and the change. Then she finished refilling a bottle of ketchup before writing the order down and giving it to the cook.

"Just wanted to tell you, I know you're busy and I know I'm hungry."

"Got it," she said.

Frank backed away from the counter and stood over George's shoulder, reading the headlines. He said, "I'm going to sit with you, Georgie. I hate to eat alone. You already order?"

"Yes," George said. He just wanted to read and look out the window.

"You never know what those waitresses remember," Frank said, winking. He set the coffee on the table and then slid into the booth heavily as if he tripped in, and the vinyl seat puffed and deflated, making a hissing noise like a tire leaking air. George didn't know what to make of Frank.

"The waitresses here are all right," George said. "They do a good job."

George put sugar in his coffee and stirred it with his knife. The only things George knew about Frank were that he didn't work and he had a fat wife named Nancy. Actually he didn't think she was that fat, just larger than most women, and larger than what most men found attractive. Nothing a diet couldn't cure.

Frank slurped his coffee and said, "Hot." Then his eyes widened and he stood, rummaging in his pockets. "I'm losing my head," he said, and held out his four quarters. "I need to feed the meter."

Frank walked across the street. He moved quickly and leaned forward, as if walking up a hill. George shook his head. "If this is retirement, I quit," he said quietly and then looked at his reflection in the window—a full head of hair gone white.

The next thing George knew, Frank swung back into the booth. George jumped.

"Didn't mean to scare you," Frank said. He breathed heavily, and his cheeks were red.

"Did you do a lap around the green?"

"It's just chilly out there." Frank cupped his hands around his coffee.

"Have you been playing much golf?" George pointed at Frank's sweater.

"I get out," Frank said.

"It's been good weather."

34

"Enough about weather," Frank said. "Nancy, my wife, said she ran into you at the store."

"Ran into her at the meat counter," George said. "It was nice to see her."

"That's what she said."

"Nancy is a nice woman," George said and felt bad for thinking she was fat, because she was nice.

Frank took a drink from his coffee and kept looking at George. Then Frank touched his lip, and there was blood on his finger.

"The cups are chipped," George said. "You've got to be careful."

"These things happen," Frank said. He blotted his lip with his napkin, which he dropped on the table, and reached for the dispenser. The waitress with the black hair came over with their food.

"Poached eggs and bacon," she said to Frank and placed the plate in front of him.

"Good work, honey," Frank said.

"It was a toughie." She tapped her pen against her head.

George smiled at the waitress. She set down his French toast and bacon.

"And some Vermont maple syrup," she said, placing a jug next to George and patting him on the back before she walked away.

"You know her?" Frank said.

"From coming in now and again."

"A regular?"

"I guess."

Frank cut his eggs and sopped them up with toast. He ate fast and wore a gold ring on his wedding finger that had a square ruby in the middle.

"A ladies' man," Frank said and chewed with his mouth open. Frank had a raised mole on his cheek. It was right in the middle of his cheek, near a wrinkle, and when he chewed, the mole moved and was almost hidden in the wrinkle. George thought it was hideous, but he couldn't stop looking at it.

"Hardly."

"She said you're friendly," Frank said and gave a tight smile. Then he pushed his plate forward and leaned into the table. He put his hand under his chin and drummed his cheek with his fingers.

"The waitress?" George looked around the diner.

"No. My wife, Nancy." Frank had some egg yolk on his chin, caught in his stubble, but George didn't say anything.

"That's nice to hear."

"Mmmm." Frank licked his fingers, wiped his mouth and hands, and placed his napkin on the table. Then he brought his foot onto his seat and retied his shoe. George couldn't see what kind of shoe Frank wore, but thought shoes said something about a man. He imagined Frank wore worn-out wingtips. He thought Frank seemed like a worn-out man.

"She said you were flirting with her, Georgie," Frank said. He kept his foot on the green vinyl seat and draped his arm over his knee. He looked like he was posing for a catalogue.

George held a piece of bacon in front of his mouth. He would never flirt with Nancy Farinella. "I wasn't flirting with anyone, Frank."

"Are you calling my wife a liar?"

"No, I'm not calling her a liar."

"Then you were flirting with my wife. Giving her the twice-over. How did it look?" Frank nodded his head and winked.

George thought of saying, "Big. It looked big."

"Frank, I was being friendly. Small-town chat." George ate his bacon and looked out the window. He scratched his nose. The leaves were orange and red and yellow and had started to fall, and the river looked black and cold. George thought Frank should be glad he was nice to Nancy. Not many men were friendly to fat women, and that was a fact.

"So how did it look?" Frank said.

"What?"

"My wife. Did you like what you saw?"

"You have a fine wife."

"You bet I do; I bet you think so."

"Frank, I don't know what you're getting at here, but I'm happily married."

TWO DAYS AGO at the meat counter, Nancy had talked about needing to find an antique pine chest, and George told her to look at Prospect Hill, off exit 11. She'd ordered pastrami, roast beef, prosciutto, and salami, and George told her to have a nice day before he walked away.

"How's the French toast?" Frank asked.

"Fine."

"I could go for a muffin and more coffee."

"I'm just about done here." George looked at his watch and tapped its face.

The waitress cleared their plates, and Frank ordered a bran muffin and more coffee. Then Frank sat back, his arms up on either side of the seat. He looked like an airplane.

"Remember those high-school dreams?" Frank said. He let his head fall back and looked up toward the ceiling. He mumbled something about old light fixtures and getting with the program of the future.

"What dreams were those, Frank?" George looked toward the counter, where chrome stools with black vinyl tops stood nailed to the floor. A small boy twirled around on one with his feet out in front of him, until his father gripped him by the arm so hard that he fell off and started to cry.

"To be a major league baseball player, the big time," Frank said.

"I don't remember that dream."

"Let me tell you something," Frank said and snapped his head up and sat forward. "I was drafted by the Detroit Tigers in 1958, but then got my ankle cracked in eight places playing football in high school, and I never played a day of baseball again."

"You were drafted by the Tigers?"

"You think I'm lying?"

"That's a hell of a thing."

"It was. It was a hell of a thing."

George thought about his old dreams. Baseball wasn't one of them. When he was in high school, he liked football and golf. He liked lakes, mountains, and women who laughed and drank beer.

The waitress brought over the bran muffin and refilled their coffees. George bet her high-school dream wasn't working in a place like Hal's.

"Excuse me," Frank said as the waitress was walking away. She turned and waited for him to say what he wanted. Frank held a thumb to his lips.

"We're talking about high-school dreams here," Frank said.

"What?" she asked. George bit his nails.

"Did you have a dream of what you wanted to be when you got older?" Frank asked, his thumb still on his lips. "I wanted to be a baseball player."

"And what did you end up being?" she asked.

"That's not important," Frank said and waved his hand at her. "What's important is what you dreamed you'd be."

She tapped her pen against her chest. She looked up and pursed her lips as if she was turning a lot of things over in her mind and couldn't settle on one. She stood there, and Frank and George watched and waited for her answer.

"Is this a trick question?" she asked.

"No, but it's a tricky one," Frank said.

"Yeah, it's tricky. I'll have to think about it," she said and walked back behind the counter.

"You think you should've asked her that?" George said.

"Everyone has a dream, Georgie. What was yours?"

George bit his nails again. Until the end of high school, he dreamed of being a senator, an army general, or a fighter pilot.

"You shouldn't bite your nails; it's bad for your teeth," Frank said.

"I've never heard that," George said and put his hands on the table.

"It's a known fact. Now, what'd you want to be?"

"I guess I wanted to be a senator."

"A senator?"

"I thought that would be prestigious and honorable. Be someone who influences laws that are passed. But I became a lawyer."

"Being a lawyer isn't bad. I always thought law was a little dry, but you must know a lot of things."

"Not enough," George said and shook his head. "What do you do again?"

"I'm retired."

"What did you retire from?"

Frank waved his hand in the air and looked out the window. "This and that and a lot of things." Then Frank took a napkin and blew his nose. It sounded like a goose call.

George wondered if *things* meant knocking people off in his younger days, shooting them from behind and dumping them near a river. Driving a black Oldsmobile and smoking. Frank had grown-up kids and a sweet, fat wife who made raspberry pies that she'd bring to Fourth of July parties at the golf course. He pictured Frank killing someone and then coming to the club to eat one of those pies.

"I saw your wife Christine yesterday," Frank said.

"Where did you see her?" George said.

"You have a nice wife."

George thought of Christine—tall and lean and fair-skinned. He wished she'd come to breakfast with him, but she stayed home to work on her paintings while the leaves were at peak color and still on the trees.

"I bet you like her," Frank said. "Husbands should like their wives."

George couldn't imagine where Frank wanted to take this. Was Frank angry with him for chatting with Nancy at the meat counter? Was he filled with regret about not being able to play for the Detroit Tigers, or was he upset because he'd played an awful game of golf three Saturdays ago during their Member-Guest

Tournament, in which George and his brother-in-law took first place?

"So, being a lawyer, you must know a lot," Frank said. "Is there anything you don't know?"

George thought for a minute. He adjusted his collar under his wool sweater.

"I don't know how to play guitar," George said.

"One more thing. There must be something else you don't know," Frank said and clucked his tongue.

George picked up the newspaper on the seat next to him and neatly folded it while he thought about what he didn't know.

"I don't know how to blow glass," George said. "I watched it once in Quechee. This guy sells his glass at high prices. It's beautiful stuff—martini glasses, vases, bowls—all this thick glass, classy glass."

"I know that place, practically hanging over a waterfall."

"That's the place."

"In Vermont."

"Right."

Frank ate the last of his muffin and gathered the crumbs on the table with the side of his hand. He made a pile. Then Frank took one last drink of his coffee and placed the mug on top of the crumbs.

"I can't stand to look at a mess," Frank said and smiled. His lip was starting to scab a little from the chip cut. "What do you say we get some air, go down by the river?"

"No thanks."

"Afraid of water?"

"No. I've got to get going."

"You think I'm sweetening up to you to take you to the river and knock you in for flirting with my wife?"

George placed the newspaper on top of the table. "I don't know. Sometimes we do crazy things."

Frank sat back, held both hands up in front of him, and said, "Who the hell do you think I am?"

"I don't know. I don't think you're that kind of guy, if that's what you're asking, but I don't know you."

"What do you mean you don't know me? We just had breakfast. Let's go sit on a bench, talk golf."

George hoped it would be too chilly to sit on a bench or even stand for long, that they'd get outside and go their separate ways. The two men took their tickets to the register. The waitress rang them up and without looking at them said, "I wanted to be a singer."

"That's a good dream," George said.

"Can you carry a tune?" Frank said.

The waitress looked at them. Her eyes were so black George couldn't find a pupil. "I can't sing a goddamn thing," she said, handing them their change. Frank left a dollar tip on the table, so George left four. As they walked out George looked at Frank's shoes. He wore beat-up white sneakers, and George felt a small victory. They weren't wingtips, but they were worn.

They walked across the street onto the center green, where there were sidewalks, benches, and maple trees. Frank walked ahead, and George noticed he was balding on the back of his head. Frank stopped in front of a bench, crossed his arms, and turned.

"Tell me who you think I am," Frank said. "I'm curious." Frank stood there, rubbing his chin like he wanted to rearrange his own face.

"Frank, I'm going home." George turned toward his car, which was parked right off the green.

"OK, let me tell you, Georgie," Frank said loudly, snapping his fingers. "I'll tell you who *you* are."

George stopped. He couldn't remember the last time someone had told him who he was. He couldn't remember the last time he'd told himself who he was. He turned back and watched Frank walk slowly toward him. Every place Frank's foot landed, there was the noise of crunching leaves. It sounded as if he were stepping on potato chips.

Frank stopped a few inches from George. George waited for Frank to say something, to tell him who he was, but Frank didn't say a thing. The two men stood there on the edge of the town green, face to face, as if about to kiss. Cars circled on the rotary, and leaves fell around them. One landed on George's shoulder.

ALL THESE LOVELY BOYS

WHEN KIRK FOUND OUT last week I might be the cameraman at the River Festival, he called, so I invited him over in the morning, since I worked afternoons. I was up early, juicing oranges and humming a tune.

"I love that song," Kirk said, walking into the kitchen. I turned and there he was, my grown son with two days' stubble in a skirt and blouse, and a black curly-haired wig. He had even penciled himself a mole above the left side of his lip.

"For Chrissakes," I said.

"Relax," Kirk said, and smoothed his blouse. It was silky and cream-colored, like something his mother had worn. I stuck the last orange on the juicer and placed the glass under the opening.

"We're just here, Kirk, you and me, no big deal for getting dressed up."

Kirk stood there and then reached under his blouse and adjusted a bra strap. "It's not dress-up."

He had a deep voice, and it scratched a little. I felt uneasy and had the impulse to punch him, almost to see if he would fight back, as if fighting would prove him a man, but I couldn't take a swing with him looking like a woman.

The dryer beeped, so I held out a glass of juice for him and he took it. I came back to the kitchen with a mound of towels and started folding them on the table. "Coffee too?" I said.

He nodded yes, drank his juice in one shot like he did as a kid, and then finished the towels while I poured some coffee.

The thing to understand here is that Kirk grew up in my house. It was his house too, so there was no reason he couldn't come and go as he pleased. He still had a room with clothes in the closet. But Hagerman Valley was small and remote, made up mostly of cattle ranchers, hunters, and corn and alfalfa farmers. Surrounding the town were thousands of acres of valleys and gorges along the Snake River, and fields full of lava rocks that looked like they'd been delivered and dumped by trucks. A man in a skirt didn't fit in.

His mother left me five years ago, when Kirk came home saying he had this thing he did, and he wanted to do it all the time. Doris cried at first, and then told him she thought he'd make a fine-looking woman. I needed more time with it, but Doris didn't have the patience. She told me I either loved my son or didn't, said she couldn't stay with a man who didn't love his son on instinct, no matter what he'd done.

I set Kirk's coffee on the table and said, "Let's go outside."

We went out back, where I kept a small garden along the fence that lined the yard. There were rocks of all sizes lying around that I planned to use as a border between grass and flowers. I'd already started laying them near the peonies, delphinium, and Asiatic lilies. I put my coffee down and started moving rocks.

"You dating?" I asked. I was never sure if Kirk was gay or straight, and instead of asking outright, I asked about his dating status, as any parent might ask their kid.

Kirk sat on the patio, his legs crossed. "I am."

I pulled up weeds and threw them on the lawn.

"A woman named Nina," he said.

"A woman with all the right parts?"

"A biological woman."

"How's that work?"

"What do you mean?"

"I mean, is she butch? Does she look like a man?"

"She looks like a woman, because she's a woman."

Don't get defensive, son. You look like a woman but you're a man. I don't know how it all works and who likes what."

There was this boulder I'd found in a field by a vineyard that Hank, my lighting man, had helped me lift into my flatbed and unload into my yard. We'd dumped it by the gate, but it was a sitting-type rock and I wanted it by the irrigation ditch that was like a creek, my own waterway traversing the property. I surveyed the thing, trying to figure how to move it.

"You might do camera for the skydiving show?" Kirk asked.

"Thinking about it."

"I'd like you to see what I do," he said.

"Haven't made up my mind." I leaned into the boulder, but it didn't budge.

"It's not a faggy thing, if you're worried," he said, and took off his heels. Then he unbuttoned the cuffs of his blouse and rolled them up above his elbows. I was surprised to see the dark hair on his forearms.

I looked at him; he didn't have makeup on except for the penciled-in mole above his lip and he looked like Kirk, the Kirk I knew: the same deep grooves of wrinkle around his mouth, the same brown eyes, the same face.

"Move over," he said, and positioned himself in front of the boulder, his hands on it, leaning in like a football player ready for the snap. "Where you want it?"

"Over there," I said, and pointed toward the ditch. "Right in front of those rose bushes."

Then Kirk rolled it into place and sat on it. He leaned over and smelled a rose. He plucked off one of the petals, rubbed it between his fingers, then threw it in the water. "Good place for a rock," he said.

Kirk performed with a skydiving troupe, but he made a living giving lessons. He helped people jump out of planes, and made sure they didn't die along the way. I always thought Kirk had talent, always thought it took courage to jump out into air, the world below him, and hope the parachute would open every time, hope nothing would be defective or stuck as the ground got closer.

Everyone in Hagerman Valley knew about Kirk; it wasn't a secret. My son dressed like a ballerina and jumped out of planes. Not the male-type ballerina—strong and catching thin, graceful women in midair—but a female-looking ballerina with a black curly wig, a lacy cardigan and a frilly tutu. He even wore those silky shoes with the hard square toe, and he wore this silver, sparkly cat-eye mask for goggles like he was at some masquerade ball.

I hummed a tune again, one I'd heard on the radio that morning, and said, "I love that song." I didn't know the name or the words but there was something about its melody, the woman's low twang; it reminded me of dust, sagebrush, and dried yellow foothills, of driving through that landscape with the car windows down.

"It's a good song," Kirk said. "You might like the song we use for our ballet."

"If it's something classical, I might not; I don't have the ear for it."

"The ear doesn't matter," he said. "It's beautiful and easy to like." Then Kirk put his heels back on, picked up our coffee mugs, and headed inside. "I have rehearsal in an hour."

I followed him in and said, "Just leave them." But he rinsed them off and put them in the dishwasher. I thought of saying something about being domestic, or being a mother, something like he'd make a good mother, and I wondered if he'd marry this Nina girl and have kids, and if then he'd go back to jeans and T-shirts, but I kept my mouth shut. He didn't need it from me.

Kirk got his purse and was ready to leave. He placed it over his shoulder. The motion seemed so natural, like he'd been carrying a purse all his life. I walked him to the door and didn't say one way or the other if I'd be there with a camera at the River Festival.

"Maybe I'll see you there," he said, buttoning his silky sleeves at the wrists.

I flicked a shiny beetle off the screened part of the door and then opened it. He leaned in and kissed me good-bye on the cheek. I let him do it. I watched him walk down the brick walkway to his car, his skirt swishing back and forth, his legs long and lean and taut with muscle. From behind you'd never know it was a man; you'd never know it was Kirk.

I wanted to meet this Nina, see what she looked like, see what kind of woman chose my son. I thought about love coming from the same places for everyone. I took the folded towels and put them in the closet and went into Kirk's bedroom. He had trophies on his bookshelf from running track in high school, mini-parachutes hanging from the ceiling, and a poster of Marilyn Monroe tacked on the wall.

I'd looked through his room before for clues as to how he got to be the way he was. In his dresser there were old T-shirts and pants, clothes he wore through high school and college. In the top drawer was a box of makeup and lacy underwear. What I would have thought to be sexy looked small and uncomfortable. Some clothes and shoes Doris left behind were in his closet; she gave him dresses and heels she no longer wore. But none of it ever told me why my son dressed like a woman.

HANK WAS STANDING but didn't need his lights until the cheerleaders came on. There was no way to light men falling from the sky. So I got my camera up and on my shoulder, and then Hank said, "You want me to do it so you can watch?"

"I got this one," I said.

"You got it."

"Drop it, Hank."

"It's dropped."

Hank stood next to me. I felt the nerves in my body. I was tight and unsettled. I tried to be an honest man—to say what was on my mind and do what I thought was right. My father always said there wasn't time in life for pretending. He said pretending to like something when you don't doesn't make you polite; it makes you a liar. I'd stuck to that, but I loved my boy and we weren't getting any younger. When it comes to your children, it doesn't always matter what you like and don't like. That said, it wasn't something I needed to have a conversation about with Hank.

The announcer came on loud over the open park space, announcing the Flying Ballerinas. People cheered and screamed and clapped, as if the men weren't somewhere in a plane trying to find the spot to jump, but were close by and could hear and know we were all waiting for them. It wasn't your usual green park with trees, but a flat stretch of land along the Snake River covered in sagebrush and junipers and sand. There was nothing between us and the sky. Music echoed off the river's canyoned walls nearby, and people hushed. I kept my camera up, on nothing but a blue sky, and waited. Waited to see my son from somewhere up above.

"This is nice," Hank said, it seemed to himself. It was classical with violins and cellos. It sounded like floating, like something moving through air. Though I'd never skydived before, the music seemed right. "Do you know this song?" Hank asked.

"Negative."

"It's fancy."

"Is there something you need to get off your chest?"

"Nada," Hank said, and pointed up to the sky.

What a sight it was to see these men come into view in white tutus, like big white snowflakes falling from the sky. There were eight ballerinas, all men, all trained skydivers. The camera wasn't catching any of it, so I set it down. I'd get them on the ground. They made circles, diamonds, and star-shaped formations. They twirled and did pliés. They goddamn danced on the air until their parachutes puffed up and out—tents of white and glitter.

The sun lit up the tulle of their tutus, and I thought, *All these glowing ballerinas*, I thought, *all these lovely boys twirling to earth*. The violins sang out over the river, and Kirk's arms were out in front of him like he was hugging someone. I held my breath. "There he is," I said. "Look at that."

"I'll never, ever bring this up again," Hank said, "but that is something else. I hate to say the word, but it's real pretty."

"Isn't it?" My lips got tight and shaky, and I felt my chin get bunched up. Kirk's toes were in a perfect point, his goggles sparkled from the sun, and I wondered if he spotted me, my boy, all bright and pretty and lovely, falling from the sky.

HOW FAR TO GO

IT'S BEEN TWO DAYS since you've talked when he comes to your window yelling he has a mango and wants you to come outside and eat it with him. You've known him for three years. You're twenty-six, you think, old enough and ready for something serious, and here he is wanting to eat a mango on a bench. It's late and you're tired. You want love, he wants to eat.

You're two floors up in a brick building, windows streetside, large heavy windows in old wood frames. When the light is on inside you can see right in—can see the woodblock print on the east wall, can see a person in almost perfect focus, can see the refrigerator with the bowl of lemons on top. He's told you he's seen your silhouette before, your breasts, the curve of your back, when you're wearing a nightgown and standing in front of the floor lamp.

You leave the windows open for air, and noises carry from the narrow street. Sometimes at night when you're in bed in the dark, talk below sounds as if people are in your apartment whispering next to you. His yelling your name to come outside for some mango sounds like an echo moving in from far off, like he's in one canyon and you're in the next, or you're on opposite sides of a quarry. You wonder if when you yell back the effect is the same, or if his name just drops down, hitting hard and flat like something wet and heavy. You think most likely it does. This is Chicago, not Paris. This is your life, not a movie.

Standing on the sidewalk, his arms above his head holding a mango, he looks desperate, small, in need. You know the mango is going to get stuck in your teeth and make a mess, but you'll go anyway, hoping maybe this will bring you closer.

"Give me a minute," you yell down, bent over, head out the window. He turns on his heel and heads for the bench across the street. You take your hair down and put on a sweater. Spring hasn't moved in yet, and the air is damp and chill, the trees still bare and leggy.

You take the stairs and walk toward him. He's wearing the striped blue oxford you gave him for Christmas. He wears it with the sleeves rolled up, and a pair of canvas Carhartts. He looks like a man who belongs in the West, with cattle and horses, and you think he's something else, sitting there cutting up the mango with a hunting knife. He's someone you could stay with.

You have been talking about taking a trip together, a drive across country and hiking in Utah. But things have been tense between you. Nothing happened in particular; there's just a gap, a lapse in things. Talk doesn't come easy. You think he's looking for someone else, someone different. He doesn't look at you like he used to, and making love is fast and rough and leaves you lonely. You want things to work out, go back to the way they've been. You love him deeply. You've loved him for years.

On the bench across from your apartment he doesn't sit close, so you keep your distance and he holds out a chunk of mango for you. You live on a quiet street with little traffic, but you hear sirens. There are always sirens in this city. He doesn't say anything, just sucks on the mango, juice dripping down his chin. You now know his window thing wasn't about romance but about being careful. About avoiding your apartment and touching. You don't know what to say these days, because you've been careful too, careful not to ask for a touch or a kiss or a talk with eye contact. You try not to talk too much because you know how easily you fall apart. But tonight you think screw it, so you start talking and you talk about anything.

You tell him how you need to have your tires rotated before driving a distance and that you've been having muscle spasms in your left thigh before bed, but that you're sure it's nothing. You haven't talked about plain things like this in a long time, and you get on a roll and feel a little full of it. You feel like speaking your mind and saying whatever you want to see how it feels, because you haven't done it in months.

He puts down the knife. He wipes his hand on his pants, then reaches for your left thigh. You almost drop your piece of mango. You feel nervous, like the first time you touched, like you're about to explode or cry or collapse.

"Your thigh shouldn't act up," he says. "You need to relax, or something must be wrong." He's leaning in to get to your left thigh, and you'd like to tell him something. You'd like to tell him you miss him, but you don't, because you're afraid he might stop touching you. He kisses you on the cheek. "You're very pretty," he says.

"We can go inside," you say.

"Let's stay out a while," he says. "I like the cool air."

You tell him how your sister started dating a fisherman who catches scallops and makes a load of money, but never pays taxes. You get worked up about it, because it's your sister. You tell him her boyfriend could go to jail for this. He's twenty-eight, and he could go down, and you wish your sister could just find a nice guy who doesn't break laws.

"Maybe he's a nice guy," he says, still touching your thigh. He's so close you can smell his hair, deodorant, breath. He smells like fruit, spices, loose tobacco.

"Maybe for now," you say.

"What do you mean for now?" He picks up his knife and what's left of the mango.

"I'm sure he's nice," you say, "but my sister's always getting herself into situations. She just gives too much away."

"That's too bad," he says and is quiet but for the noise of his knife splitting through the mango, like a shovel going into dirt.

You want him to touch you again. You want his affection. Even though things aren't good, you want him to claim you, tell you no one else can have you but him.

"I think my sister could do better," you say a little loudly, "find someone better."

"Calm down," he says. "Maybe it's not your place to worry about it."

You take a bite of mango and feel it in your teeth in places you can't reach, and you're not about to stick your finger in your mouth to dig it out. You sit still, looking straight ahead.

"You just get so loud," he says.

"I'm calm," you say. "What, are you worried someone might hear me?"

He laughs and says, "Actually," and doesn't even look at you. You feel hurt, a tightening in your chest, and breathing doesn't come easy. You feel your eyes getting full, and this isn't what you wanted, not today, and you're so tired. You're tired of being an embarrassment. He used to love that you'd talk about anything, get loud and excited, and sometimes swear. But now you're crass and embarrassing, and this isn't the first time he's let you know it.

"There's no one around," you say.

"That's not the point."

"Then forget it." You drop your piece of mango on the ground.

"Forget what?" he says, now looking at you, still holding the knife in one hand and half a mango in the other.

You stand facing him on the bench. Your hands are wet and sticky from the fruit and you don't know where to put them, so you hold them down at your sides, careful they don't touch your clothes. "This," you say, "this whole thing with us and that mango. This is such a mess."

53

You hold your hands out toward him, palms up. "I wasn't an embarrassment before. It's like being embarrassed of your mother, and it's awful. I think this is it."

He puts the knife and mango down on the sidewalk and reaches for your hands. You let him hold them, and he says, "I don't understand."

You consider letting him hold your hands and telling him you don't know what you're talking about. You consider telling him you're tired, then inviting him inside. You don't want things to end, but they can't go on this way.

"You don't understand," you say, and move your hands from his.

He wants to know if you're still on for driving across country and hiking in Utah. You tell him maybe; you tell him to call you tomorrow. You go back to your apartment alone to wash your hands and go to sleep. Before you change, you turn out your lights. You peek out. He's not on the bench, so you open your window and look down the street. You see him walking in the middle of the road, slowly. You feel bad for what you said, but you had to say something. You had to let him know you might not be around forever.

A week later you meet after work and go to a bookstore together to look through travel guides on New Mexico, Colorado, and Utah. You talk about going to Anasazi ruins and Valley of the Gods, eating corned beef hash and drinking beer by a campfire. You want to do this, and you think it can't be too bad. There will be time alone together, and time to talk. Maybe you can work on being friends, at least being honest so you don't have to be too careful with your words.

You look once more at the pictures of southern Utah, the red-rock mesas and wide, dry canyons. You imagine the quiet and the stars at night. You imagine lying side by side in sleeping bags, and him falling in love with you again in the middle of nowhere.

"Let's go," you say, almost a whisper.

"Good," he says, patting your shoulder, leaving his hand there a minute. "Good."

"I'll get food for the drive," you say.

"I'll bring a flask and some bourbon for camping."

"I think we'll need it."

You wonder what you'll do about hotel rooms and beds on the drive out and back. You haven't planned where to stop along the way; he wants to play it by ear. All you know is you're heading to the Southwest and he wants to make it there in under seventy-two hours. The day after the mango he called, and you told him you couldn't stay physical, that it would drive you crazy and you'd feel cheap. He took it seriously, and you regret that. You thought it would make him come to you, but he hasn't.

The next weekend you meet at his place to load his truck with backpacks, sleeping bags, water bottles, and a Coleman camp stove. You bring music for the ride, and pretzels and soda and books to read out loud: books on history and disease and stories of men hunting in the South. He wears his hunting knife on his belt and loans you a Leatherman to wear on yours. You thank him and put it in your backpack. Next thing you know, he's putting on a fur hat with earflaps.

"What the hell is that?" you say.

"You've never seen one of these? It's Russian, from Siberia."

You've seen them before but never knew he had one. You leave it alone and figure he's excited for camping and the wilderness.

You're not an hour into the drive when you move some tapes around and he gets snippy.

"They're just tapes," you say.

"They're my tapes," he says, "and I want them where they are."

You sit back and watch out the window, wondering why you thought this would work. You're driving through rural Illinois, and it's been raining on and off all day. You see a thunderhead from miles away. The land being mostly flat and farms and fields, you can see a lot of things coming. You wonder if you saw this coming and just ignored it, if this falling out of love was sudden or just feels sudden. You wonder if there was anything you could have done, but you don't know where to start.

He tells you he wants to drive through New Mexico to see his aunt and uncle. You ask what they are like. His aunt rides her horse in the summer with a pistol to shoot rattlesnakes and wild dogs. She used to be a bush pilot in Africa. She breeds horses that come from Norway. Hardy, stocky horses the color of straw. His uncle is a retired architect and designed their house and knows about Pueblo ruins and artifacts, and places to hike in the Southwest. You tell him they sound nice and interesting, but you stay quiet otherwise. You don't know people like his aunt and uncle.

He tells you he wants to go to downtown Santa Fe too, to buy a silver belt buckle maybe for his father or maybe for himself. "The Native Americans set out handmade jewelry on the street. Maybe you'll find something you like," he says.

"Maybe."

"Maybe a pretty bracelet or necklace," he says.

"It's not jewelry I need," you say.

"OK," he says, and turns up the music.

You keep the atlas on your side of the truck. You don't like surprises and don't like getting lost. You ask which way you're going, and he tells you: south and then west, I-55 to I-44 to I-40. You follow the states with your finger as he talks: Illinois, Missouri, Oklahoma, Texas, New Mexico. You flip to the states and track the drive to know exactly where you're going, noting national forests, mountain ranges, and rivers.

He's still wearing the Siberian hat. People in passing cars slow down and point.

"Isn't your head getting hot?" you say.

"My head is fine," he says. "Everything is great."

AFTER TWO DAYS of driving you arrive at his aunt and uncle's ranch outside Santa Fe. They give you the guesthouse, with everything you need: a kitchen, bathroom, sitting room, and two bedrooms. They leave you alone and tell you to rest up before dinner. You've been to New Mexico before. You came in college with girlfriends and stayed for twenty dollars a night in a motel in Albuquerque that had a vibrating bed, and no bolt or chain on the door.

But you have never been to New Mexico like this. The ranch is six thousand acres; there is a gate and a mile-long driveway that leads to the white adobe house where the Pecos River cuts through the land behind it. You're glad you came here and that he is of these people. You're in the bathroom when he yells from the bedroom he's going to take a walk.

"I'd like to go," you say.

"Hurry up," he says.

You come out of the bathroom, and he's sitting on the bed with his boots, coat, hat, and gloves on.

"Just a minute," you say, and go through your bag for wool socks. You sit next to him and put on your socks and lace up your boots. You're surprised he doesn't get up to walk around the room. Instead, he hands you your hat and gloves and you thank him. As you walk out the sliding doors you put on your hat.

"You look like an Eskimo," he says, and pats you on the head.

You think maybe things are turning. Maybe this trip was what you needed after all.

You walk toward the stables, and three horses come to the fence. You take off your glove and run your hand down a horse's nose and back up between its ears. It's warm and soft, and the smell reminds you of riding when you were younger and lived in the East. You've always loved the smell of hay and leather and dirt.

"I love horses," you say, but he's already walking.

You follow on a dirt path through silver sagebrush. You keep your eyes on the ground, watching for rocks and plants you don't know the names for, all brown, dry, and dead. You look up when you can; the hills are tall and round, and you wonder what is beyond them.

You want to talk but can't think of anything to say. You start to open your mouth and make a noise, but then cough and stay quiet. It's OK to be quiet, you think; there's nothing wrong with that. So you keep walking and concentrate on the sound of your feet moving over the land. Sounds of leaves crackling like breaking sticks, and the ground smelling dusty and wet at the same time. You make it to the top of a ridge, and you both stand there and look around. The sky is flat and solid white, and your face is cold.

"This is nice," he says, smiling.

"It is," you say.

"I'd take this place any day."

"So would I."

It starts to snow, so you turn around and walk back to the house. He walks ahead of you, and you don't say anything about it. You just watch the snow fall around him and wish he would walk by your side without your having to ask.

He tells you he is going into Santa Fe and will be back soon. You stay in the guesthouse and look at watercolor paintings of rose-colored deserts, broken mesas, and horses on the walls; you flip through a coffee table book on New Mexico, and another on Pueblo Indians, birds, and petroglyphs. There are beams of wood on the ceiling, holding the house in place. Everything feels old and special, like something you'll never have. You can't sit still and wish you were tired enough for a nap, tired enough to shut your eyes and forget this feeling of want, this feeling of reaching into a dark space for something solid to hold onto. You make yourself sit in the chair, and you stare at a painting of a red barn in winter. Everything white but the barn and two pine trees. Everything so quiet.

Two hours go by, and he's still not back. You feel like you're hiding out, so you walk over to the main house. It is white adobe with wood beams, and the floors are deep-red Mexican tiles. You feel uncomfortable being alone, being among strangers, but you go anyway, telling yourself to grow up. You find his aunt in the living room reading by the fire.

She doesn't hear you come in, so you stand there and say hello. She turns and says, "How was Santa Fe?"

"I didn't go."

"Have you eaten lunch?" She closes her book and keeps it in her lap.

"No, but I'm fine, thank you."

You sit in a chair on the other side of the coffee table, not sure if you're intruding.

"Are you having a good time?" she asks.

"Yes. Very nice."

You look out the window and rub your hands on your thighs. "You have a beautiful ranch," you say.

She's looking out the window too and doesn't say anything. You wonder if you weren't supposed to say that, or if maybe she just didn't hear you. It is quiet, and all you hear is the fire crackling and popping.

"How did you get into breeding horses?" you ask.

She sighs and takes off her reading glasses. You're sitting with your hands between your legs. You want her to tell you a story filled with passion for horses, that she's always loved them and wanted to raise them. That this is a dream come true. That she goes out to feed them, brush them, and ride them every day just because she can.

"We had all this land and thought we should have horses on it," she says.

"Did you ride when you were younger?"

"A little," she says, "because my mother thought I should."

"I used to ride," you say. "I love horses."

She smiles a fake smile and blinks slowly. She doesn't ask you anything about what you like or where you come from, and you wonder if it runs in the family.

"I'll let you get back to your reading," you say.

"We'll have dinner at seven," she says.

You go back to the guesthouse and wish you had stayed there all along.

You hear a car pull up and pretend you've been reading this

whole time. You don't want to appear as if you've been waiting. But he doesn't come in, so you go to the other house and hear him talking to his aunt. He has bags and is saying how he found a great burrito place to eat lunch.

"How was Santa Fe?" you ask.

"Look at this," he says, smiling, and pulls a silver-and-turquoise belt buckle out of its wrapping.

"It's nice. Is it for your dad?"

"I also got this bracelet for my sister," he says, holding a silver band embedded with stones in reds and blues and purples.

"She'll like that," his aunt says.

You wonder if he knows he does this. You wonder if he actually listens but chooses not to answer.

Before dinner you take a shower. When you come out of the bathroom a turquoise bracelet is on top of your clothes. He pretends to read in the armchair. You pick it up and touch the stones.

"Put it on," he says.

"Thank you," you say, and you mean it.

At dinner you drink red wine and eat lamb. You talk about books and films and places you have visited in Europe. He is nice at dinner and listens when you talk, laughs at your jokes. You feel charming. You're thankful for the wine and the distraction of other people. He looks at you across the table in a way he hasn't for months, gentle and steady, and you feel beautiful and hopeful in the candlelight. He's always loved the way wine gives color to your face. It's almost as if he's sad for how things are and he's watching you as if he's wanting you back. You look at the turquoise bracelet on your wrist and it slides a little to the side, almost big enough to fall off. He looks at the bracelet too and reaches across the table, pushing it upright, and says, "With a little bending it will be a perfect fit."

You're leaving the next morning for southern Utah, to hike and camp for four days so you ask his uncle for suggestions. His uncle brings out topographical maps and describes the geography of places. You both choose Comb Ridge because it is closer to the

Four Corners and Valley of the Gods. You help his uncle clear the table while he goes outside with his aunt to smoke. Through the window you see the orange embers of two cigarettes burning, and watch them move away down toward the river.

His uncle is tall with a white beard. You rinse, and he waits for you to hand him the next dish to dry.

"I think you're all right," his uncle says.

You smile.

"He's just got his head in his ass."

"Something's got his head, and it's not me," you say.

Then he lifts a dish up high, and drops it on the tile. It hits with a loud clap and breaks into pieces. He jumps back and laughs. "By God, that felt good." He points at the dish scattered on the floor. "Don't make it your business to try to fix him."

Then you pick up a dish and hold it high too. You're not sure you should do it; it's not your dish or your house. But his uncle's smiling at you, so you let go, let it fall. He whoops like a cowboy.

"There you go," he says. "Plate slipped, shit happens."

You laugh and double over. You laugh so hard you cry.

You step over the shards of porcelain toward his uncle, and they make a crunching noise under your shoes.

"Careful now," he says. "Where're you headed?"

You give his uncle a hug. He's still for a moment, and then hugs you, wraps his arms around you and pulls your head to his chest.

"Oh," he says, "I miss my girls. Girls have such a sense about them." He rests his chin on your head, and pats you on the back. He reminds you of your grandfather, not breaking the hug until he's ready. But that's all right, because you feel safe. "Thank you for that," he says.

"Let me help clean this mess." You step back and bend down to pick up pieces of dish.

"Nonsense," he says, and knocks on your back like a door. "Go get some sleep."

You stand outside the guesthouse in the snow watching the Pecos River. There's a full moon and shadows on the ground and light coming off the water. You wish for something like this some-day: an adobe house in the middle of nowhere on land covered with sagebrush, yucca plants, and piñon trees; horses in stables; and a river. But none of it will matter unless you have someone to love. You want someone to grow old with. You know no matter how much you love him, he is not yours to piece together. This man you love like no other is not yours to have. You go inside without turning on any lights. He's in his bedroom, kneeling on the hearth and fussing with kindling, building a fire. His bed is a double. You don't want to sleep alone.

"I've always wanted a bedroom with a fireplace." You feel your cheeks warming. The flames blaze quickly; he knows how to build a good fire. The room is aglow with flickering light; the dry wood pops and crackles.

"Your lucky night," he says.

"I just want to sit and watch the fire a while."

The window is open and the room smells like cold and wood smoke. The air feels smaller. He undresses and gets under the covers and says, "You can stay."

You take off your shoes and coat and sit on the bed next to him. He's lying down facing you. You know you won't go with him to Utah, sleep under stars or drink beer in a canyon. You won't go with him anywhere again. You look at his neck and shoulders, the smoothness of his skin, and you feel something deep inside you falling. You touch his hair, and he closes his eyes. His fine, brown hair is so soft. He doesn't push you away, but shakes as if there is some current going through him, sneaking up his spine and into his head, settling him still and quiet. You touch his face, trace his eyes, nose, and mouth with your fingers. They are lines and curves you want to remember. You lean down and kiss him, and he kisses you back. You feel it in your bones, in the back of your head, in your feet. Your arms feel numb. You kiss so slowly, lips brushing and pressing, it feels like you're both mouthing words. Words too sad for either of you to speak.

I'LL TELL YOU WHAT

Jimmy's father always told him what, always said, "I'll tell you what," and then his father would tell him things. His father told him thousands of things, maybe millions.

When Jimmy was twelve he stood five foot eight. Most girls thought he was sixteen, so Jimmy had girls looking and whispering at him when he went shopping with his mother, or sat and ate hot fudge sundaes with his father at the Dairy Queen hut off Route 7, the main road into town. Jimmy didn't mind the girls looking. Those older girls weren't making fun of Jimmy, but wishing he'd talk to them like he was a sixteen-year-old boy, but he didn't, because he wasn't. What did he know about girls? He still kissed his parents and believed what they told him. He still rode a bike with streamers on the handles, and let his mother buy him sweaters with Izod alligators stitched on them. He never talked to the older girls, just looked and smiled, and those girls would blush and bow their heads and touch their hair.

Jimmy's father sat on the bumper of the car, ate a dish of blackberry ice cream, and watched and smiled too and said, "I'll tell you what, Jimmy, you've got to be careful not to break girls' hearts when you get to their age. They break easy, almost too easy if you ask me, but that's just the way it is, so you're going to have to get used to it."

"OK," Jimmy said.

"You remember that."

"I will."

"You keep that in your head for later," Jimmy's father said, pointing his folded paper napkin at Jimmy's face.

"Yep." Jimmy looked out to the road, watched the cars passing, and spooned up his melted ice cream, dripping some on his knee and his shoe.

"What did I say?"

"Hearts break easy." A drop of hot fudge had landed on Jimmy's thigh and looked like a freckle the shape of Texas.

"Girl hearts," his father said.

Jimmy looked at his father. There were mosquitoes buzzing around his father's head, and one stuck in his hair.

"You got a bug in your head," Jimmy said.

His father swatted at it and said, "Jesus." Then he looked at his hand and wiped it on the side of his shorts.

Jimmy was still looking at him. His father's chest was sunburned and red where his T-shirt opened at the buttons. His chest hair poked out, and Jimmy wondered if he'd have some like it one day. He wondered if it was itchy to have hair on your chest.

"Does it matter if it's girl hearts or boy hearts?"

"Of course it matters, Jimmy. Girl hearts break because boy hearts are so tough, and sometimes the toughness hurts the girl and beats up at her heart. Like breaking someone's arm by accident, and then it gets better. It's just like an arm."

"Oh," Jimmy said, putting his empty plastic cup on the hood of the car. Then he fingered the chocolate off his thigh and ate it.

"Yeah," his father said, "oh is right. I'll tell you what. You'll be saying oh a lot when you get older too. Get used to saying oh, and uh-oh, and oh no, and oh yes, and if you're lucky, oh God."

"OK," Jimmy said, but he didn't know all the ohs he'd say in life, or what they'd mean when he'd say them.

"Good ice cream tonight—it really hit the spot." His father took their cups and threw them in the trash by the takeout window.

The girls still watched Jimmy and his father. The girls shifted their hips while they stood and licked ice cream off cones and spoons, poked at each other, and covered their mouths while they said things Jimmy and his father couldn't hear. The girls were tall and lean and smooth-skinned. Jimmy's father came back to the car and winked at Jimmy.

"You've got a lot coming your way, Jimmy, you lucky kid." His father shook his head and said, "Jesus, you just wait a few years."

Jimmy didn't know what his father was talking about. He knew nothing about girls except what his mother told him: not to hit them, not to call them names unless they were nice names like pretty or smart, and not to touch them anywhere but their hands. Jimmy spent a lot of time thinking about hands in home-room and during recess. He tried to look at all the girls' hands he could, and was a little afraid of them—they often had color on the nails, pinks and purples and sparkly blues all chipped up and peeling.

But later that year when their class was watching a movie in the gym, Susie Stevens touched his hand, then ran her fingers all over the inside of his palm, and he felt his breathing get fast and his palm get warm, and his chest tickled inside him. Jimmy decided touching hands was good like his mother said it was, and he tried to touch as many girls' hands as he could from that moment on. Some were round and some were thin, but they were always soft. Jimmy loved girls' hands.

When Jimmy was fourteen, his mother told him not to touch girls unless he was sure they wanted him to. At the same time Jimmy's father was still telling him what. And this time he told him he was still lucky, and that all the pretty girls would give him things without him even asking for them. It was winter and cold, with six inches of snow on the ground. Jimmy and his father were shoveling the front walkway.

"They'll look at you when you're not looking, and they'll listen to songs and think about you," his father said.

"I know that," Jimmy said.

"Did you know they'll lay in their beds at night and pretend they're kissing you?" His father held the shovel by his side, leaning on it like a crutch, and gave Jimmy a wide-eyed look.

"How do you know?" Jimmy kept shoveling.

"I just know."

"Who cares?"

"I'll tell you who cares—you will. It's going to be on you to make the first move and kiss them, because that's the way it is. The boy has to take the girl from thinking things up late at night to doing them sometime, somewhere."

"I don't know," Jimmy said.

"What don't you know?"

Jimmy stopped shoveling and looked at his father. "Won't they just say when they want to do something?" Jimmy wiped his forehead on his coat. It was cold, but the shoveling made him sweat. Jimmy wasn't sure he wanted girls to give him things without asking.

"They won't say a goddamn thing. All they'll do is get real quiet and look at their hands and laugh a little." His father leaned his shovel against the house and clapped his gloves together, and snow fell from them.

"Laugh?"

"Because they don't know what else to do. It's nerves." He took off his gloves and held them in one hand.

"Jesus," Jimmy said.

"Jesus is right, and I'll tell you what," he said, flapping his gloves at Jimmy's face, "when you kiss for the first time you'll be saying Jesus, and then you'll say it after, and then you'll pray to him you can do it again. A lot of Jesus in your future, son, a lot of Jesus."

"What kind of things are we talking about?" Jimmy's friends talked, but Jimmy wasn't sure what was true and what wasn't. None of his friends had ever seen a real naked body up close. Some had felt under sweaters, and some between legs, but they didn't really know what was what. Jimmy's mother didn't allow sex movies in the house, and his father didn't argue, because he would watch them on cable when he stayed in hotel rooms on business. Jimmy had seen those kinds of movies at friends' houses late at night in finished basements, but still, Jimmy didn't really know what his father meant when he said *things*.

"Things," his father said, and seemed to be remembering them, looking up at the flat gray winter sky.

"What if I don't want things?" Jimmy wasn't sure.

Jimmy liked the looks of the full-figured women in the movies, how their cleavage bunched up under tight sweaters, and he imagined what it might be like to be in the same room with one of those women, who wouldn't talk to him, just take off her clothes and let him do whatever he wanted. He knew a woman like that wasn't going to show up knocking on his door one night. Sure, Jimmy thought about sex, and felt up a girl once at a party in a dark closet while playing Truth or Dare. But he didn't have a girlfriend. So he stuck to hands, and that seemed all he could take, with the way his chest busted all up from a smooth hand on his. He thought with anything else he might explode.

"You want things, Jimmy. Things are good," his father said, holding his arms out wide, as if things were all around them, and as big as the whole wide world.

"You make it some mysterious mystery."

"It is. You'll know what I'm saying here when you get your brain on right and stop touching girls on their hands all day and night."

"I like hands," Jimmy said, turning red.

"Your mother is a lovely woman, Jimmy, but listen; I didn't marry your mother by holding her hand, and we didn't get you by holding hands."

"I don't want to know anything about you and Mom."

His father put his gloves back on and scraped the porch steps.

"Sounds like you don't want to know anything about anything," his father said, pushing the snow from the steps onto the walkway in front of Jimmy. "There'll only be so many things that'll matter in your life, and the girls you love will be one of them." He pushed the bill of his hat up and looked straight at Jimmy. Steam came from his forehead as if a fire had been put out, as if it were a sign that he knew what he was talking about and Jimmy should listen.

But Jimmy had started to doubt his parents, started to think he was smarter than they were. Jimmy didn't let his mother buy him sweaters with stitched-on alligators anymore, and now Jimmy rode a dirt bike and a skateboard. But this time he listened to his father. It was something about the steam rising from his forehead, girls and love, and so many things that matter in life. Jimmy listened and thought about how he lay in bed at night and fantasized about kissing, like his father said girls did, and Jimmy thought he wanted to know something. He wanted to know things.

When Jimmy was fifteen, he took Holly Pinter into the woods. She had skin tan and smooth as an apricot, and shiny hair. He liked her mouth, round and red, and he wanted to kiss it. They sat on old dry leaves on the ground, and she looked at her hands and laughed as his father said girls did when their nerves got going, and then he leaned in and kissed her. His hands were on the ground next to her, holding him up, and her hands were in her lap holding each other. Jimmy left hands out of it, and felt something different. He felt something open up, like his father's arms held up and out that day in the snow, as if this was what things were—a space being made inside his chest, big and wide, with room for feelings to enter and bang around inside him like a crazy ball bouncing inside a box.

Jimmy's father knew he and Holly kissed. He saw them kissing outside the garage when he came out to get the mower one afternoon. That night, his father looked at Jimmy from across the dinner table and smiled and nodded. Later that night, his father came into Jimmy's room and leaned in the doorway.

"What did I tell you?"

"Turn down my music?" Jimmy said, and moved toward his stereo.

"About girls," he said.

"They're all right," Jimmy said, not looking at his father's face.

Now that Jimmy was fifteen and in high school, he didn't tell his parents much, except where he was going and when and where his baseball games were.

"That Holly seems all right."

"She's all right."

"Are things good?"

"Things are good."

"That's how they should be. Jesus, that's how they should be." And his father tapped on the door and walked away.

Jimmy loved Holly. When he was sixteen she was the first girl he saw naked up close, and he touched her like glass, soft and careful and slow, to make sure he knew what was what. He loved to feel her move against his skin. Jimmy had his driver's license and a beat-up station wagon, and found fields and apple orchards where Holly and he could be alone. At sixteen, Jimmy stood six feet tall, and girls thought he was eighteen. But Holly knew he was sixteen, and he knew he was sixteen, and that was all that mattered. Sweet sixteen, Jimmy thought, and things are good. He knew this was what his father had talked about: Holly was a girl who'd matter in his life.

But then a woman named Lucia thought Jimmy was eighteen and told him she would give him things. She was twenty and didn't look at her hands or laugh. She wore red lipstick and tank tops, and Jimmy thought, Jesus, and found himself saying, Oh God. Jimmy would say her name, "Loosha," quietly over and over, like water in his mouth, "Loosha," and she kept giving him things without his asking. Jimmy didn't tell Holly, but she found out.

She came to his house with a wet face and blurry eyes and told Jimmy he had broken her heart.

"Hearts break," he said. "Girl hearts break too easy." Jimmy stood in his driveway kicking at the gravel.

"Fuck you," Holly said, and walked away. Jimmy heard a door in the garage close, so he stayed outside. He didn't want his mother asking questions, so he sat on the back lawn and picked at the grass. Then Jimmy drove around and went past the fields and orchards where he took Holly, and his chest tightened and felt smaller. He didn't want the things Lucia gave him anymore.

When Jimmy got home, his father and mother sat at the kitchen table. His father looked up at Jimmy and said, "Let's go for a drive."

Jimmy didn't argue. They got into the car and backed out of the driveway without talking. The gravel sounded like tires over hard-packed snow.

"I could get an ice cream," his father said.

"Sure," Jimmy said, and rolled down his window and laid his hand on the side mirror. Trees were green and full, and a yellow light like butter cut long shadows on lawns.

Jimmy got a hot fudge sundae, and his father got a bowl of blackberry ice cream. "Like old times," his father said, and leaned on the hood. Jimmy leaned on the hood too. The metal was warm, and the engine ticked.

"Listen, I'll tell you what," his father said and opened his mouth, as if about to speak, but then put his hand on Jimmy's shoulder. "I don't know what to tell you."

MAN IS THE MEASURE
OF ALL THINGS

THE VANDERMIES INVITED Russell to their house in Ketchum for dinner. He drove on a dirt road that wound through the base of mountains that looked so smooth of sand they might slide down from the smallest movement upon them. It was dark and cool in the valley, but the sun was high, still on the tops of the hills and mountains where they would hike up to for dinner. He'd been here many times while working on the house, but he was still unsure of landmarks and turns; he looked for the wooden walk bridge that crossed over the Lost River half a mile before their driveway. The river ran to his right; birds flew back and forth over the road, low and fast, seeming to just miss the car by chance or luck. He came around a bend, sure the bridge was less than a mile away. Then, just ahead, Russell saw two four-wheelers on the rocky berm. There was a man waving him to stop.

Russell pulled over and rolled down his window. "What is it?"

"We've lost one," the short hairy man said. "We've lost one, and you've got to help."

"Lost what?" Russell said.

Another man, red-haired and large, came up from a dip behind the embankment and said, "I can't see a goddamn thing. Can't see or hear or nothing."

Russell stayed in the car. The men wore worn canvas pants and long-sleeve shirts in the heat. They were tough, Russell thought. Men who could stand the heat in those clothes killed things, fixed busted engines, and spat on people if they felt like it.

"Is this an emergency? Can I call someone?" Russell stopped himself before he held up his cell phone. They already knew he wasn't tough; he didn't have to prove it. He wore a short-sleeve collared shirt and khakis. He hoped they couldn't see the leather loafers he wore without socks. He'd bought them that day at a men's store he'd never been in because of the prices. But when the Vandermies invited him for dinner, he knew the crowd would be wealthy, and it was his chance to make an impression.

"We don't have time for that. We need your help," the short man said.

"What I mean is, is this serious, is someone hurt?"

"It's serious," the redhead said, "or we wouldn't be asking for help."

"It's just that I have a dinner to get to; people are waiting for me," Russell said, pointing in front of him, as if people were down the road waving for him to hurry.

The short man walked toward the car. Russell hit the automatic lock and pushed in the clutch.

"Look, Jack," the short man said, standing in front of the open driver's side window. "Get out of your car and help us find what's missing." He stood close enough that Russell smelled his bourbon breath.

"My name isn't Jack," Russell said. "What are you two doing?"

The redhead cradled a shotgun, and spat chewing tobacco from the side of his mouth.

"Get out of the car, Jack. We need help," the short man said, touching Russell's shoulder as if they were pals who'd just had a fight and were making up.

"To find the last person you shot?" Russell said, and laughed nervously, a snort.

"Funny, Jack. Good one. Let's go—we've got to eat dinner tonight too."

Russell thought about getting out to help with whatever awful mess they had made. He knew some survival skills from an EMT course in college, but that was twenty years ago.

The short, hairy man was still leaning against the car when Russell let out the clutch, his heart beating so fast he could hardly breathe or feel his arms or legs. He peeled out, tailing and sliding on the dirt. He was sure he was saving his life. He looked into the rearview mirror but couldn't see anything through the dust cloud. He never heard a gunshot. Russell thought they must have expected him to cave in once he saw the gun and get out of the car like a fool. Forget it. He wasn't dying that day.

He just wanted to pass the wooden walk bridge, get to their house, and get the hell up the mountain to have some wine and red meat with a bunch of rich people who might hire him to work on their homes. He needed new clients. He had a wife and five-year-old daughter. He had to feed them, pay the bills, save money to send Olivia to college. If he didn't get more clients soon, and pull in two thousand more a month, he'd have to get a nine-to-fiver. He'd have to go back to working a shitty job as a teller at Cold Creek Bank just to make ends meet.

When Russell pulled into the Vandermies' driveway he was winded, as if he'd been running. He turned off the engine and sat. I'm alive, he thought. I might not be alive if I had waited another minute. He looked around and found his backpack. In it were two bottles of California Zinfandel to carry up as gifts, and swimming trunks for the hot springs on their property, a fleece jacket, a camera, and a box of newly printed business cards. He lifted the pack to the front and held it in his lap.

Russell eyed his glove compartment, where he kept a pack of Marlboro Reds. He hadn't smoked in three weeks. He didn't want to smoke anymore or die from cancer, because he was responsible for Olivia, but it made him feel better just knowing the pack was there in case of emergency.

"Fuck it," he said out loud, and took the cigarettes and put them in his backpack. Russell thought a glass of wine and a cigarette would calm him down at the top of the mountain. That was just what he needed.

Russell walked toward the house and saw John Vandermies coming down the trail. Russell waved and took a deep breath. He didn't know if he should tell him about the men on the road; he didn't want to scare anyone and ruin the evening. The Vandermies were a prominent family in town, and it wasn't every day he got invited to their house for dinner. But this night he did, because he'd done some renovations for them. He put in new bathrooms with deep cedar Japanese-style soaking tubs, green glass wall tiles, and glazed concrete floors with hints of burgundy swirled throughout. John called him an artist of the home, and invited him to meet the right people. "These are the clients you want," John had told him. "People with money falling out of their pockets."

"Russell Parker," John said, with his hand out to shake. "We've been meaning to have you over for some time. I'm sorry Isa couldn't make it."

"Our daughter has bad poison ivy."

"Unlucky," John said. "Don't want to infect a sitter."

"And Isa wants to make sure she doesn't scratch and get scars."

"Life will scar her soon enough, won't it?" John slapped Russell on the back.

"Soon enough, Russell said, and wiped his forehead with a bandana. He couldn't stop sweating. John headed toward the trail, and Russell stopped.

"Did you forget something?" John said.

Russell walked back to his car and locked it.

"Nothing to worry about out here," John said.

"In case of bear," Russell said.

"Is your car an automatic?"

"No."

"Then you don't have to worry."

"OK," Russell said. "Well, it's locked anyhow."

John stood smiling, so Russell smiled back. John was athletic and strong, his hair going white. Russell guessed he was close to sixty but looking good.

"The house looks great, John."

"Many thanks to you, Monsieur Artist. We'll show you how it has shaped up when we come down after dinner for a soak."

Russell hoped John wouldn't call him Monsieur Artist all night. The name was fruity, and besides, though he was there to network, he didn't want to be known as the renovator all night. He wanted to feel like a rich man for once. For just one night.

When they got to the top of the trail, Russell shook hands with the other company, who looked clean and well dressed for having hiked up a small mountain. They all stood around the firepit with glasses of wine and tans. In their white and khaki pants and cable-knit sweaters, they looked like people who played tennis and golf. John handed Russell a stemmed glass and told the group how Russell had locked his car in case of bears, and how he'd told him he didn't have to worry since his car wasn't an automatic, and that Russell believed him. Everyone laughed, and Russell smiled and thought John didn't need to be an asshole about it. He wondered if telling him about the men on the road with shotguns would make him sing a different tune. Then maybe John would jog down the mountain to lock his house. But Russell didn't want to say anything; he already felt like a klutz among these tennis types.

Russell turned and looked out over The Pioneer mountains. The sun lined up to go down between two peaks, like in the movies. Russell chuckled to himself and wondered how the rich got it all, even the sunsets. He lit a cigarette and was glad he was invited, and even a little glad Isa stayed home with their daughter. Russell felt good to be there with people he didn't know well, all of them bronzed and handshake-polite, and he felt important and wished for these people to wonder who he was and want to find out.

He stood with his head high, looking out over the valley, and pretended all this was his. He thought there was nothing wrong with having goals, something to work toward, and nothing wrong with wanting to be rich. He could see down the sloping valley to the river and the dirt road he came in on. He scanned for the men on the four-wheelers, but he didn't see anyone. They'd probably left, or found some other sorry fool to stop and help them. Maybe he was nervous about coming up here and had overreacted. Maybe the men were just drunk and aggressive about finding some wildlife they shot. Another glass of wine and he wouldn't give two shits if those guys came up the mountain. Surely John Vandermies would pull his weight, give them some grilled lamb and calm them down.

"Hello there, Mr. Russell," said Elaine Chalmers. She was tall and lean, and walked toward him carrying a glass of white wine she held in front of her as one might hold a tissue, as though her glass was light and fluffy and something she might throw off to the side at any moment. Six months earlier he'd salvaged wide pine boards from an old barn in Vermont, refinished them, and put them in as flooring in her five-thousand-square-foot cabin.

"Hello, Elaine," Russell said.

"Russell," she said, and touched him on the shoulder. Her gold bracelets clinked. "So good to see you."

She wore a white blouse unbuttoned low. Russell could see the lace of a white bra through her shirt.

She tilted her head to one side and brushed her hair out of her eyes. "Let's sit down."

They sat in foldable canvas chairs.

"I'm so sick of these people," she said. "They're a bunch of fakes. It's nice to see a person with a real job and life. How is your real life?"

"The real life of the working class is just fine. Nothing glamorous. Are the pine plank floors holding up?"

"Oh, yes. I tell everyone you're a good lay." She raised her eyebrows and smiled.

"Whatever brings in the business, Elaine."

She put her hand on his thigh. "My, you're warm."

"The hike up," Russell said.

Elaine was not married. She'd had two husbands, and left them after having a child with each, taking half their money with her. Everyone in Ketchum and Sun Valley knew she was set for life, and was the kind of woman who announced what she wanted and then got it. She wouldn't get it with Russell, though. Russell loved his wife and his daughter; he wasn't a cheater or a sleep-your-way-to-the-top kind of guy, and even though she was rich as hell, he wished Elaine would take her hand off his thigh.

"You generate a lot of heat," Elaine said.

"Elaine." He scooped up her hand and lifted it like a wounded bird. "Let's behave." He placed her hand on the armrest.

"Oh, please," she said. "Spare me." She stood and strode to a group of others. Within minutes they all craned their necks, looked at him and laughed, throwing their heads back, their mouths open, some wiping tears from their eyes. Elaine winked at Russell and held up her glass. He faked a smile and lifted his glass toward her, and wondered what was wrong with these people. Did having money make them narcissistic assholes, or was this just who they were? Were there rich assholes attracting rich assholes atop hills and mountains all over the world?

A motor echoed below, and he knew it was the four-wheelers. The rev and low rumble came closer. Russell felt as though a swarm of bees flew into his chest.

"Monsieur Artist," John called, and waved Russell to join him. He held a bottle of red wine and stood by the cool, dark former mountain-lion cave he'd had Russell smooth out, seal, fit for a door, and then outfit as a wine cellar. He poured wine into Russell's glass and said, "Cheers, Russell. These men need renovations, and I told them you're the man for the job."

"Peter Harvey." A man held out his hand and Russell shook it. "I love John's cement floors. I want the same floors. Can we bargain?"

The skid of sand and crunch of twigs and sagebrush under the tires of the four-wheelers approached. Russell flinched. Didn't anyone else hear the noise? Russell wondered if he should run. Run now. Run for his life.

"Don't be a cheap bastard, Pete," John said. "You make in an hour what it costs for one of those floors."

"We can bargain," Russell said, "but first I need to take a leak." He wanted to get out of there. Survival instinct. His body was ready to run. Adrenaline coursed through his veins. His senses were as high as they'd ever been. He felt like an animal. He turned toward the woods, but Pete grabbed his upper arm.

"Hell, I won't cheat you out of full price. I just like to negotiate. It's what I do." Pete slapped him on the back with his other hand.

Russell smelled the four-wheelers' exhaust. It caught in the back of his throat.

"All right. Full price then." Russell leaned back to get free, but Pete held his grip.

"I prosecute people. Put them away for life. Do you know what it's like to have that power?" He didn't even look at Russell when he spoke, but up toward the sky, as though his thoughts were inspired from the gods. Who did this guy think he was, Caesar? Jesus Fucking Christ?

"I build things," Russell said. "I don't determine anyone's future but my own."

"Good man," Pete said. "That's an honest answer and an honest living."

"It's the only answer I got."

The hum and rev was just below the rise of the hill and the dinner party.

"I'll tell you what that power is like." Pete's grip tightened; it felt like the blood-pressure cuff at the doctor's. Tight. He felt his blood stopping where Pete pressed. It hurt.

"Before you tell me anything," Russell said, "you need to let go of your death grip or I'm going to piss on your loafers."

"I'm sorry," Pete said. "I got caught up. Go, go." When he released Russell's arm there was a rush through his biceps: blood flow restored. Russell's hand was pins and needles. He shook out his arm; Pete had practically put it to sleep. Russell walked quickly behind the cougar cave, toward the stand of cottonwoods and larger boulders where he could hide. His foot slipped on sandy ground going up a small incline, and he fell on his knee.

"Aw, fuck," he said. Red wine splattered on his pant leg like drops of blood. He kept the wineglass with him; he figured he could break off a shard to use as a blade.

"Careful there, buddy!" Pete yelled.

"I got it," Russell said. "Just a slip."

"Or too much wine?" John laughed and slapped Peter's back, and he laughed too.

"Shut the fuck up," Russell said under his breath. He wasn't sure why these rich people kept laughing at him. He didn't see what was so hilarious about being afraid of a bear, not wanting to cheat on your wife, or falling on your knee.

Russell got up the embankment and moved deeper into the darkness of the trees. "Now we'll see who's laughing, you bunch of wine-sipping ass-faces," Russell said, looking down at the crowd. Though no one could see him, he flicked them off with his middle finger. Then he crouched behind a boulder and thought about his wife.

Isa had been tired, distant, and crabby the past six months, but he didn't take it personally. Having a kid and a job was exhausting; he was tired and crabby too. Neither of them got enough sleep, or had enough sex or any time to themselves. Three weeks ago, as Russell hurriedly pulled on his boots to get to work, he'd bumped into the nightstand and dislodged from Isa's copy of the *The Great Gatsby*, which she was teaching in her eleventh-grade class, one of those loose scraps she used as bookmarks. On it was a phone number and the name *Nathaniel*. Isa taught at the private Community School; the richer the kids the more issues they had. She called parents daily. He hadn't given it a second thought; it was probably some kid's dad.

But now Russell squatted behind the rock and thought, *Nathaniel Nathaniel Nathaniel, who the fuck is Nathaniel?* The name reminded him of Faneuil Hall in Boston, Daniel Boone and a coonskin cap, and reading Hawthorne's *The Scarlet Letter* and his English teacher asking, *"Whether hatred and love be not the same thing at bottom?"* In high school, he thought hate and love were too far apart—one violent and one sweet—so he wrote a four-page essay and got a C on it. But after ten years of marriage and a child, he thought perhaps, at bottom, they were the same. He loved Isa. He loved her so much that if Nathaniel were someone other than a parent, if he were someone she was fucking, someone who could ruin the life they had together, someone she loved, then yes, he could hate her for it. Hate her because he loved her, and maybe only because he loved her. Survival instincts, that was all there was to it. It was all about staying alive and keeping what you loved and what you needed.

The red four-wheeler crested the hill, dust pluming behind as it bounced and rushed over sagebrush and rocks toward the party. Russell waited, he wasn't sure what for. The moment was uncertain. The sky darkened. Streaks of orange tracked through the sky like flames. The circle of tiki-torch flames flicked and waved. He smelled citronella. A bat dove and turned just in front of his face, and he felt the wind from its wings and its tiny black leathery body. He leaned his forehead against the rock, and it was bumpy and cold. Was Isa screwing some one else? Was that why they hadn't touched in months? Why was he scared and hiding behind a rock in the dark? His gut said, *Get off the mountain and go home now.* It was the same voice that told him to let up the clutch and drive up the mountain. And so which was it—did he want to be up or down this mountain? Was he willing to work for these arrogant, condescending kind of people? His legs tingled from crouching. He lifted his head above the rock. No one had moved or seemed concerned. Elaine's bangles glinted gold against the firelight.

Russell was raised in Missoula. His father and grandfather took him and his two brothers hunting in the fall and camping in the Bob Marshall Wilderness in summer. He knew how to hunt and kill bear, deer, duck, and chukars. He knew these types of men; they were the type in his family: drinking, reckless, angry, fighting. Men he'd left behind long ago. The kind of man he chose not to be. But they were inside him, not far beneath the surface; they were in his DNA.

The four-wheelers parked in front of the fire, and the engines cut. The chatter and clinking glasses continued as before. The woods darkened. Russell was sure no one could see him, so he stood to get a better look.

The big red-haired man waved John Vandermies over. "We have something for you," he said and raised his eyebrows. John walked toward the men and shook their hands.

"We lost one, "the red-haired man said, "but we found the other two."

Jesus, Russell thought, did they kill dinner?

The men lifted a blue tarp from a trailer hauled behind one of the four-wheelers. There were two teenage boys gagged and tied on the flatbed. They squirmed and flailed like fish on land.

Elaine Chalmers gasped. Pete Harvey looked at John with a cocked head and bunched lips. The group circled around the boys and blocked his view. Russell stuck his hand inside his wineglass and pulled back, breaking off a piece. He put the palm-sized jagged glass in his pocket and carried the broken stem down toward the fire.

"No need to panic," John announced to the group, and everyone hushed for an explanation. He pointed to the short hairy man and the big redhead. "These fellows help me keep my land in order." Then he pointed to the two boys. One had blond hair and the other had brown. "And these hooligans were stealing, and I wanted a chance to meet them personally. I apologize it had to happen in the middle of our gathering, but we've been looking for them for two days."

"What did they steal?" a voice called from the crowd.

"Why don't you ungag them," John said to his men, "so they can tell everyone what they've stolen."

The men ungagged the boys. Then they stopped squirming and were quiet. They were scared.

Russell stepped forward into the firelight. The red-haired man looked right at him. "Oh, hello," he said.

Russell's grip on the glass tightened. He felt the sting of a cut on his finger.

"You know each other?" John asked.

"We've crossed paths." The redhead winked at Russell. Then he slapped each boy on the side of his head. "Tell them what you stole."

"What *did* we steal?" the brown-haired boy said.

John stepped closer. "Yes, boy. What did you take that doesn't belong to you?"

"You can't do this. This is illegal. We didn't *steal* anything," the blond said.

The men looked at John. John took a sip of wine and kept his eyes on the boys. He shook his head back and forth. "Stealing is illegal."

"We didn't steal anything," the brown-haired boy said.

Russell tilted his head sideways to get a better look and recognized the brown-haired boy. His nose was slim and pointy like a shorebird's. He was one of Isa's students: a poet, a cross-country skier. His name was Tucker. Then Russell looked back at John, who was smug and smiling.

"They're just kids," Russell said. "Let it go, John. I know this kid. He's my wife's student."

"You know this kid?" John asked and pointed at Tucker.

"Hi, Tucker. I'm Mrs. Parker's husband."

Tucker smiled crookedly, confused.

"This is insane," Russell said and looked at John. "You never did anything stupid when you were young?"

"No, I didn't."

The red-haired man's lip curled, and he spat dip from the side of his mouth. Then he put his finger over his lips and said, "Shhhhhh."

Tears ran down Tucker's cheek. Russell felt the violence rise in himself. He felt his father and uncles, he felt the ugly impulse, the electricity in his arms and legs.

"None of you are going to say anything? You're OK with this?" Russell asked, looking around.

People backed away from the four-wheelers, behind the tiki torches, and into the shadows, as though if they couldn't be seen then they didn't need to have an opinion. They could look the other way, because they could afford to.

"Relax," a voice said from the dark of the crowd.

"He has two boys who go to school with your kids bound and gagged on the back of a wagon."

"Nnnnn." The redhead grunted, spat dip again, and wiped his mouth on his sleeve.

"Step off, Russell," John said. "This isn't your business."

"We're not like their kids," Tucker said. His voice cracked. "Our parents work three shitty jobs to send us to that school. We live in Gooding. And their kids . . ." he stopped.

"Quit your crying," John said.

"What did you steal?" Pete Harvey stepped forward, as if in court.

"Yeah, what did you do?" a voice cried out from the dark.

Everyone waited. The fire embers popped and floated into the night above. John shifted from one foot to the other, and his nose twitched. Elaine Chalmers coughed. A throat cleared. Someone put a hand on Russell's shoulder from behind to draw him back, as if to say, *It's not worth it. Let it go. Join us.* Russell dropped the shard of glass, and he wanted to go home—now. He wanted to get back to Isa and his daughter. He wanted to know all was OK, and make sure they were cared for, safe, his, but he did not step back. Tucker and the other boy lay on their backs, looking up at the sky. The tiki torches created a ring of fire, and the only ones inside it were Russell, the two men with the four-wheelers, and the boys who were tied up like animals. Defenseless. Waiting to be told what they deserved and what the world thought of them.

WHAT WILL MAKE THIS
ALL RIGHT

WE WERE ON OUR WAY to brunch at the Hill House. A nice place for brunch: Victorian, all red velvet and brass inside, and they served a good omelet. It was a perfect October Saturday— cool and crisp, a bright-blue sky and maple trees bursting full of orange and red leaves.

On the drive to town Charlotte said, "Rick, stop at the store."

"Can't we go after we eat?"

"We'll be lazy after we eat. I want to buy decorations for the front porch."

"Charlotte, I'm starving."

"We need something for the photographer. You just want us and a plain black door in the picture?"

Us and a black door was fine with me, but Charlotte had ambitious ideas for our first Christmas card. She'd hired a photographer to come take our picture at one o'clock, and she'd already been working on a form letter for two weeks, carefully thinking of ways to present our lives to family and friends. She asked me to think of interesting things we'd done for her to write about.

In the hall closet Charlotte kept a basket full of Christmas cards featuring our friends' family pictures on front porches with wreaths hanging behind them, and there was always a black Lab or golden retriever in the center or just off to the side. These cards came with typed and crisply folded letters recounting their year's high points: ski trip to Vail, stocks doing well, Joey took his first step, Mary scored two goals, Peter is a straight-A student, promotion to vice president, cycling trip in Italy, wine-tasting in Napa Valley, God Bless, Peace to All. In just a month or so, all these praise-songs to the good life would again start massing in their mailbox. More scenic shots of Tuscany from the saddle of a bike; snaps of a beaming friend with a new baby or of a line of children with toothy smiles, all in coordinated outfits. And the sentences about promotions, fancy trips, private schools. Charlotte stared at the photos and pored over the letters for details she might have missed. Then she'd comment: *They already have three boys! They own a brownstone in Park Slope! Look how beautiful Cali is! She's thin and has such shiny hair!*

Some people called Charlotte and me late bloomers. I'd met her in graduate school, where we studied to become residential architects. We were married at thirty-two, but we felt so young, just out of graduate school, getting used to a life of work and responsibility. At thirty-five we designed and built our own house in a nice rural area of Massachusetts where we could afford two acres. Charlotte hung a pine wreath on our front door over the holidays, and we started trying to have a family. Before we knew it we were thirty-seven. Charlotte's mother said sometimes the first time takes a while. It had taken her mother two years to get pregnant with Charlotte.

"Supermarket, Rick, on your right. Please?"

"We can stop," I said, and turned into the lot. This picture meant a lot to her. She'd already picked out what we should wear, swept the front porch; she'd even washed the door and windows that morning. I'd raked and bagged leaves the day before. If she wanted me to wear a green sweater and khakis that afternoon and smile on my front porch for an hour, it was the least I could do. If she wanted to stop at the store for cornstalks and pumpkins, no problem. I loved Charlotte. I loved that she wanted us to have a family, and wanted to send out bragging Christmas cards.

The fall decorations in front of the store's sliding doors looked festive. "I love this time of year," she said. "Maybe we can carve pumpkins later." She laughed and clapped. I liked it when she laughed; it made me want to kiss her. A strand of her auburn hair fell across her eyes, and I wanted to reach over and push it back, touch her face. Then she looked like she was holding her breath, and as I watched her face like that, sort of still and tight, I lost track of where I was going. Then her eyes widened. I swiveled my head back to the windshield but it was too late. I smacked into a shopping cart, and it went skidding into a car, a black sedan with a dog in it. The cart hit the door, bounced off, then settled in place. The dog went nuts, barked its head off like the cart was an attacker, a metal attacker on wheels.

"Oh, no," she said.

"Shut up," I said under my breath.

"Me?" Charlotte said.

"The dog."

"It's just scared," she said, "just doing what dogs do."

"I'm sorry, I'm just hungry."

I parked right in front of the black sedan, because I wasn't thinking with all the barking. Charlotte inspected the side of the sedan for damage.

"It looks all right," she said. "Those old cars are like tanks." Then she tapped on the window and told the dog to calm down. "Shhh," she said. "Everything's all right, buddy." She had her face up close, practically touching the glass.

"Come on, honey. Let's do what we need to do."

"I feel bad for the dog. We scared him to death."

"He'll survive," I said, and walked toward the store.

We got a cart, and Charlotte filled it with five pumpkins, two cornstalks. She took her time; everything needed to be perfect. She held up two bunches of Indian corn. One was red and white, the other was yellow and purple. "Which would look better against the black door?" she said.

"I like the purple and yellow."

She inspected both by holding them up in the light, laying them on the asphalt, and then she chose the red and white bunch.

"OK," she said. "We're ready."

We went in to pay. The bakery was killing me with doughnut and cake smells everywhere. The place was packed for a Saturday morning, as if a hurricane or winter storm were coming. We stood in the checkout line and Charlotte still looked like she was holding her breath. She had this grimace on her face and then rummaged through her purse.

"I have money," I said, but she wasn't listening.

"I'll be right back," she said.

The cashier lady was quick, and I started hefting the pumpkins onto the conveyor. The woman in front of me was large and slow and held a little blond boy on her hip. She set him on the counter, and he poked at the cashier's face and pulled at the small purple glasses she wore, until she said, "No, no, you cute piece of heaven."

The big woman looked at her kid and said, "Crap, Timmy, leave her alone." She tore through her pockets, looking for money. I turned to look at the magazine rack, and I fingered some candy on the shelf and put my hand over my own pocket for my wallet, but it wasn't there. I patted all my pockets, but nothing. My wallet was in the car.

Charlotte came back and put a box of tampons on the belt. My heart felt jammed in my throat, like a chunk of apple had gone down the wrong pipe. Charlotte breathed loudly through her nose, shrugged, and looked beyond me out the window.

"Do you have your wallet?" I asked.

She shook her head no. My ears tingled. All the voices, metal cart noises, and beeping registers were too loud, and when I looked at the floor to calm my nerves I saw a twenty-dollar bill sailing out of the big woman's pocket right in front of me. It floated back and forth and twirled to the floor. She didn't notice, and I didn't say anything. She paid, hoisted the kid on her hip, and left. Charlotte saw it too and seemed in a trance, as though it were a feather fallen from an eagle.

The cashier weighed our pumpkins and kept pressing the wrong code. She started over three times. I bit my lip to keep my mouth shut. Finally, she rang us up, and the bag boy put the pumpkins back in the cart.

I couldn't stand the idea of being in there one more minute, so I bent over, picked up the twenty, and handed it to the cashier.

Some guy behind us said, "That's not your money, mister."

"The hell it's not," I said.

"I saw it fall out of that lady's pocket," he said. He was young, maybe in college, and held a case of beer under his arm.

"Were you waiting to pick it up," I said, "a little beer money to go get shithoused tonight?"

"What's your problem?" he said, and his nostrils flared.

"What's this?" The cashier said.

Charlotte put her hand on my arm and turned around, calm and steady. "Listen," she said to the young guy, "it's his money. That's my husband's money, and we're using it to buy pumpkins and cornstalks and Indian corn and tampons." She didn't take her eyes off him. He stared back at her, scrunched up his lips while shaking his head and then looked away.

Charlotte turned and smiled at the cashier. "Look, I don't mean to be rude, but we're getting a Christmas family photo taken this afternoon, and we have to get set up at the house."

"I'm sorry about that." She handed Charlotte the change, leaned in, and whispered, "I know you didn't steal anything. You aren't needful people."

"Thank you," Charlotte said.

We got to the car to load the pumpkins and cornstalks in the trunk. A wind blew, and leaves and dirt twirled in the lot. The leaves sounded like paper moving over the pavement. Charlotte's hair whipped around her face, and some stuck to her lip. It was already eleven; we had two hours before the photographer showed up.

"I am needful, Rick. I have needs," Charlotte said and opened the back door. I hefted pumpkins onto the seats. "Put them on the floor, honey, or they'll roll off and their handles will break."

I secured them on the floor behind the front seats, where they wouldn't budge.

"See? I am bossy and needful," she said. "The worst thing anyone could ever be."

"Charlotte, you're fine. You know things and say them out loud. You want what almost every person wants in life. We'll keep trying."

She crossed her arms over her chest and shook her head. She did this when she was about to cry and didn't want to. "And look at that dog," she said. "That poor little dog stuck in there." She walked toward the car to take another look at the dog, who sat and watched us from the driver's seat.

"Let's go home," I said. "Screw brunch. I'll make us something to eat. Some scrambled eggs and bacon."

Then a man with a tweed blazer and wire-rimmed glasses walked up and pointed to the black sedan. "I saw it happen," he said, and then pointed at the supermarket. "I saw the cart hit my car from inside."

He was younger than us, and I was surprised the car was his. It looked like something he'd inherited from a grandparent.

"We looked over your car," I said. "My wife was saying earlier how these old cars are like tanks, and they are—we couldn't find a scrape on her."

The man opened the door and let the dog out. It jumped on my legs, a big brown Lab. I petted it, then pushed it off me.

"That's a nice dog," Charlotte said. "Hey, buddy." She clapped her hands, and the dog ran to her. She petted it on the head.

"You can have the dog," he said. "For hitting my car, you get a dog."

I wondered where the hell this guy had been hiding out, waiting for us to come back. "There's no dent or scrape," I said. "We checked."

The man licked his finger and ran it over his door, then pointed at something. "Right here," he said. "There's a line."

I walked to where he stood. I squatted to get a good look, and the dog jumped on my back. There was a small line, but it was too low to have come from the shopping cart. "That's not from me," I said.

"Looks like Ruby likes you," he said.

"I'm sorry," I said to the man, "but we can't take your dog."

"Look," he said. "I'm supposed to be at the vet right now killing this perfectly good dog. Instead I've been driving around with her all morning. She's a perfectly good dog, only two years old. My daughter just kept poking at her eyes and Ruby snapped."

"Is she trained?" Charlotte said.

"Sit," the man said, and Ruby sat. Then the man walked over to us and said, "Come," and Ruby walked over to him.

"Not bad," Charlotte said.

"Just keep your fingers away from her eyes," he said.

"I think it's time we had a dog," Charlotte said, and then she bent down and looked into Ruby's face. "Do you want to live with us? You're a nice girl."

The man looked at me and raised his eyebrows. "Looks like this is settled, then." He reached into his backseat, pulled out a leash, and handed it to me. "She has all her shots, and she's been fixed."

"Honey?" I said. "Come on, we can't do this."

"It's perfect timing," Charlotte said. "She can be in the picture with us."

Charlotte seemed happy, and I didn't want to argue in front of this guy. I opened the back door, and Ruby jumped in. Then Charlotte and I sat in the car and watched the man drive away.

"We have a dog," I said. Ruby poked her head between us, and she smelled like a wet, dirty sock. I rolled down my window.

Charlotte looked over at me, smiled, and her eyes were full of tears that hadn't fallen yet. "I don't know what I'm doing," she said. "I'm sorry. I just feel all fucked up and old and late in this life."

"What's more fucked up is this huge brown dog in our backseat, and she stinks," I said.

Charlotte laughed a little. Then her tears fell.

I pulled out of the lot and got us going on the main road back home, past white clapboard houses that had already put out cornstalks and pumpkins. The road was bumpy from ice heaves, and loose change shook in the cup holders like bells. We wound up and down small hills where maple trees burned red and looked like giant apples set against the green. Ruby lay in the backseat and seemed right at home with us, as if we'd had a dog for a long time.

"How about in our Christmas letter we tell people about our camping trip in Maine last summer?" I said. "Tell them about that lake we canoed at five in the morning, with all the mist rising up. Tell them about sitting naked in the biggest hot-spring pool we've ever seen, with all the volcanic mountains rising around us like a moonscape in Iceland."

She was quiet and sat with her hands between her legs.

"Write about the beautiful house we designed using cedar and bamboo from Japan and clay tiles we bought in Vietnam, about all our skylights, and how we can sit in our bathtub and watch the stars. Write that we just saved a brown Lab named Ruby in our local grocery-store parking lot. Tell them that we've spent eight wonderful years together. Tell them how much I love you."

She shook her head yes and touched my shoulder. Her hand was so warm I felt like weeping. What could I give her that would make all this all right? We didn't expect others to understand our heartache, our empty sadness, since we were blessed in so many other ways. I kept my eyes on the road. "Tell them we have everything we want, Charlotte. We'll smile so fucking big in that picture, we'll look happier than ever. They'll think we're right where we want to be."

She kept her hand on my shoulder. I felt like it could sink right into me, through flesh and bone. Reach down deep and grab my heart out.

Ruby snorted and began pawing furiously at the backseat like it was a mound of dirt. Her nails were small hooks, and they pulled and tore at the leather.

"Jesus," I said. "Are you serious?"

Charlotte twisted her torso and shoved her body through the two front seats toward the back, trying to grab Ruby's collar. "Ruby. Ruby."

But Ruby dodged her. Ruby was practiced.

"Goddamnit, dog," Charlotte said. "Rick, pull over."

I pulled onto the shoulder, next to Mack Hill Farm and its pumpkin patch. Charlotte got out, opened the back door, and Ruby jumped into the way back. I heard crunching.

"Not the cornstalks," Charlotte said. "Now she's standing on the cornstalks."

I turned to look at the backseat, the stretched and slit mess of leather. There was a thin birch near the car, and I thought for a moment we could tie Ruby to that tree and leave.

"Could you help?" Charlotte said. "She's ruining everything."

"I'd be happy to." I walked to the hatchback. "Charlotte, you guard the backseat and don't let her up there." Charlotte sat in the rear seat and watched me. I opened the hatchback, and Ruby jumped out and hopped up and down on the pavement like she wanted me to throw a stick.

"Rick, I didn't know the dog was crazy," Charlotte said. Her face was red and her hair tousled, and I could tell she regretted this dog. The whole idea.

"What do you want me to do, Charlotte? We took her. She's ours."

In the field a tractor rumbled along with a flatbed full of parents and kids sitting on the back, on their way to pick pumpkins.

"OK, Ruby," I said, and opened the back door. "No screwing around." She jumped up, and I grabbed her collar. Charlotte frowned at me. I led Ruby's head to Charlotte. "Hold her by the collar and keep her calm while I drive."

"This poor seat." Charlotte ran her hand over the leather. "I'm so sorry, Rick."

"Forget it," I said. I pulled onto the road, and as I did, everyone from the tractor waved at us. They bumped along between rows of large orange globes, waving and smiling in anticipation of what they would pick out to take home with them.

"Hello good-bye," Charlotte said and waved from the backseat, as though she were saying hello to the reality of our lives and good-bye to what she'd imagined and hoped our lives would become.

Ruby sat at the window and barked at the families. I was weak from hunger, and all I wanted was to be full.

SANCTUARY

I HAD A DATE for the first time in a year. It was mid-June, and I was meeting Rob at the Corkscrew Swamp Sanctuary.

Every Sunday between May and August the sanctuary opened evenings to allow visitors to see and hear birds you wouldn't otherwise. The sanctuary was one of my favorite places: there were miles of wooden boardwalks through swampland where giant leather ferns and Boston ferns fanned over the ground in soft greens, and where red and orange lichens covered tree trunks. Old-growth bald cypress trees rose from shallow waters, Spanish moss draped over branches like gauzy webs; pink and white hibiscus bloomed delicate and wide. A lush tangle of beauty—this was what Florida looked like before all the concrete, roads, and developments. This was what I wished it still looked like.

I was excited for our date. I had liked Rob for months. That spring he took the six-week black-and-white photography work-shop for adults I taught at the local arts center in Naples. His photos were lovely, simple and clear. He focused on portraits, which was what I loved the most—people's faces and capturing a feeling, a personality. I took a portrait of each student in the studio and developed the photos as part of our homework exercise. His photo was alarming. His eyes were dark shiny jewels looking straight into the camera. I imagined him complex and honest and tender. I wanted to love him.

I met Rob by the Animal Sightings board, where people wrote down what they saw, where and what time, like *alligator on a rock in the lettuce lake at 2:00 p.m.* He looked wrecked the closer I got. Red, puffy eyes like he'd been crying.

"Is everything all right?" I asked.

"I tried to call," he said, "but there was no answer. I didn't want you to get here and think I stood you up."

He turned and leaned on the walkway railing, and beyond him a heron opened up its wings, which were longer than I expected from such a tall, skinny bird, and it lifted into the air. Rob squatted and put his hands on the boardwalk. He had the body of a swimmer, strong and shaped. I had a hard time not looking at his arms, which were smooth and tan and had lines of muscle and vein.

I touched his shoulder. "What happened? Is there something I can do?"

The sun lowered in the sky, still a ways from setting, and a stretch of pink and orange clouds reflected on the marsh waters. Huge fanned saw palmettos glowed as if lit from within. I thought of touching my hand to the top of his head, his fine hair that curled at the edges. Instead I squatted so that my eyes met his.

"My brother died, and I have to identify him," he said. He looked up at the sky, his eyes full and glassy, and took in a sharp breath. "I'm no good," he said. "Can you drive me there?"

MY RADIO WAS BUSTED, so on the drive I kept the windows down. It was a hot and humid evening, but the air felt good. The noise of wind was like rushing water, and loud enough that we didn't have to talk. Rob kept his arm on the window frame and held the side mirror with his hand. He watched everything to our right: flatland, cabbage palms, and open sawgrass marsh. The little bit of untouched land that would inevitably be bought, filled, and built upon. It seemed possible the sanctuary might end up the last place in Florida for all the birds to live.

We were close to town.

"Where are we headed?" I asked.

"Could we stop at my house? The funeral home asked that I bring a photo of Dan and I forgot."

He directed me through lights, rights and lefts. His place was a bungalow with light-blue shuttered windows, within walking distance to the beach.

"My grandparents left this to my brother and me," he said, as if it were the first thing he told everyone who walked up the slate walkway; a two-bedroom this close to town and the water was worth well over a million.

"Lucky you," I said.

"Yeah, lucky me. Now I have it all to myself."

"I didn't mean that; I'm sorry."

"No, Dan was a slob and he never did the dishes." He walked through the kitchen into his bedroom. He had dark marks of sweat on his blue Oxford near his shoulderblades and down his lower back. I stayed in the living room.

It was cool in the air conditioning. The furniture looked passed down from his grandparents along with the house. The floors were dark hardwood and the couch and chairs sturdy carved teak with bright green and white cushions. There was a black lacquered Asian armoire in a corner, and a gold Japanese silk screen with painted mountains, cranes, and bamboo trees on it. It covered a whole wall.

Rob walked in with a photo sticking out of his shirt pocket. I could only see light-brown curls and dark eyes. "My grandparents lived in Japan and traveled in Southeast Asia." He swept his hand around the room. "I could use a drink. Can I get you a drink?"

"Should we go for your brother?"

"They said anytime before eight." He walked to the kitchen and opened cabinets. He set two tumblers on the counter, filled them with ice, and poured Maker's Mark. He rolled the sleeves of his shirt to his elbows and came in with the drinks. "Have a seat," he said. "Dan's dead; what's the rush?" Ice cubes shifted and clinked in our glasses. Light broke through the window onto his drink and cast a honey-colored watery glint on the wall. I wanted to say something. I wanted to say, "I wish your brother hadn't died," or simply, "I am so sorry." But I felt at a loss, and I felt like an idiot, with a blank brain, nothing to tell this man on one of the worst days of his life.

I took a drink and felt the trail of whiskey down to my gut. I wore a lime-colored sundress and felt like a frog in the middle of a lilypad on the couch by myself. My shoulders were smooth and tanned, and I'd hoped he'd notice and want to touch them. Push the strap of my dress off my shoulder and kiss me there. But he sat in the deep teak chair across from me, a glass and bamboo coffee table between us, his brother dead and waiting.

"This is awkward," I said.

"Yes," he said, "yes it is. That's why we're drinking."

"Is there someone I or you can call? Someone you know well?"

"Absolutely not. Do you know how my brother died?"

"I'm not a psychic." I took off my flip-flops and folded my legs underneath me.

"I'll tell you because I hardly know you. He died at an amusement park." He took a drink, then choked laughing. He put his drink down and laughed so hard his face was deep red and his eyes watered. He took a handkerchief from his pocket and blew his nose and wiped his eyes. "He was on the teacup ride, that thing that spins while spinning around. They said his teacup went apeshit, came loose and flew off the platform like a fucking tornado." He laughed and laughed and gasped, "A flying saucer!"

I laughed; I couldn't help it. It was an awful and ridiculous way to die. He got up and came back with a bowl of ice and the bottle. He poured two more drinks and sat next to me. The sun set and the room went dark, but I could still see his face. Everything else was a shadow shape in the room.

"Why was he at the amusement park?" I asked.

"That's the sad part of the story," he said. He took the photo out of his pocket and set it in front of me. His face was close to mine. He still had heat to him, even in the coolness of the room.

"He was a thirty-three-year-old man in love with an eighteen-year-old girl." He leaned back and crossed his legs. "She wanted him to win her a stuffed animal. She wanted him to go to her senior prom. He was mad about this girl, Britt. He would have done anything for her."

"Is that so sad?"

"Are you kidding me? Who at his age is hanging out at an amusement park unless it's with his own kids?" He drank his whiskey in two swallows.

I lifted the photo of Dan close to my face. It was a snapshot at sunset of him on the beach. He looked older than Rob, but very much the same, with olive skin, a sharp, angled face and rosebud lips. I thought, *At least he was in love.* "I'm sorry you didn't like her."

"It wasn't that I didn't like her," he said. His arm and shoulder leaned into mine, and he pointed to the picture. He smelled like water and spice. I wanted to stay in the house as it darkened. I wanted to keep drinking and to lie down and touch all night. "She was too young, not very smart, a little trashy." He put his hand on my thigh and kissed my neck. His stubble tickled my skin.

"You can't predict who you'll fall in love with," I said.

He turned my head toward him. "Maybe," he said. He looked directly at me for the first time all night, and seemed confused, as if he were searching for someone else. I wondered whom he deeply loved and wished for. Then his eyes shifted onto my shoulder, then out the window behind me. He sat back and looked at his watch. "I guess there's no point in talking about this," he said. "What's done is done." He ran his finger over my shoulder. A clock ticked loudly from somewhere in the room.

"One big fucking surprise after another," I said.

"What's that?"

"Life." I untangled my legs from underneath me, and knew this wasn't going anywhere. For so long I'd wanted to fall in love and be loved, to find some kind of normalcy with a partner, but all I seemed to meet were men in the middle of catastrophes. I was not perfect. I was not easy. I was older. But I was still pretty. I still had time.

"Let's get this over with," Rob said. He stood, put the picture back in his pocket, and held open the front door. He waited in the yellow of his porchlight and looked straight outside at who knows what—a bougainvillea plant? Palm tree? Grass? I felt horrible about his brother, but I wanted him to look at me. I wanted someone, some man, to look at me. To see me.

IT WAS 8:00 P.M. when we got to the Eternal Light Funeral Home. I was buzzed and hungry. The funeral home was red carpet everywhere. Wreaths of fake red and white roses hung on the four viewing-room doors that lined the hallway.

"Mr. Raynor, Bill Raynor, is the guy we're looking for," Rob said.

It was my second time to a funeral home, and it creeped me out. I'd never seen a dead person before. Every dead person I knew had been cremated.

A man in a white lab coat sauntered out of an office eating lo mein from a Chinese takeout box. It smelled so good.

"Mr. Raynor?" Rob stood.

"I'm your man," Mr. Raynor said.

"My brother is here. Accident at the amusement park."

"What a shame." Mr. Raynor nodded his head down the hall, walked in that direction, and we followed. "Sorry to eat on the go." He clicked his chopsticks together. "It got late."

I looked at Rob and raised my eyebrows. What was wrong with this man? It seemed days and night with the dead made him forget how to talk to the living.

We went downstairs into a room full of display coffins for sale. Some were opened and some were closed. They had black, brown, and deep-red shiny outsides and satiny colored insides in reds, pinks, light blues, yellows, and whites like a jockey's uniform. Then we walked through to what looked like an operating room: a bright light above, a porcelain table, scissors, scalpel, and other instruments on a small stand nearby. Metal and glass cabinets, linoleum floors. Everything the color of gunmetal gray and sea-foam green.

Mr. Raynor opened a tall white cabinet and pulled out a metal rack with a black body bag on it.

"Is he a mess? Can you give me a minute?" Rob said.

"No one's ever ready for this," Mr. Raynor said and unzipped the bag so fast we didn't have time to turn or think. "Time of death was 12:34 p.m. I cleaned him up as best I could."

Rob put his hand on my elbow, and we moved closer to his brother. I expected a smashed and bloody face, torn limbs, total destruction. But he looked all right. He looked like he'd been in a fight or fallen down. There were stitches in his lower lip and some on the right side of his head behind his ear. His body was bruised and scraped, and there were some deeper cuts on his arms and legs. He looked like a beat-up guy taking a nap. I reached out and touched his chest. It was cold and hard and felt like chicken skin just out of the refrigerated package.

"Once we embalm, he warms and loosens up," Mr. Raynor said.

"What killed him?" Rob said.

"Impact, head trauma." Mr. Raynor pointed to the stitches and light brusing behind the ear and hair.

Rob took the photo from his pocket and laid it on Dan's chest. I looked at his face in the picture, then at his face lying in front of me, and it seemed entirely possible Dan would open his eyes and say something. The idea of brain and organs shutting down, of breath stopping and a soul moving on, made no sense. Where did he go?

"He's a handsome guy," Mr. Raynor said. "I'll make him look just like that picture. And you'll want to bring in something for him to wear."

"What a waste." Rob put his hand on Dan's forehead as if taking his temperature and whispered, *So cold.*

"I'm sorry for your loss," Mr. Raynor said. "You can never know anything in this life."

Rob touched Dan's hair by his temple—round curls, fine and thin—and he twirled one around his forefinger. Dan's hand was tan and right in front of me, and looked as if it might reach for something any minute. I tried not to move and breathed as lightly as possible. Everything was quiet and still. I became overwhelmed with missing my mother and father right then; it was an unexpected ache that moved up through my body like an animal. I didn't want them to ever die. I didn't want to die. I still hadn't figured out the reason I was alive. There was so much to do. So many people to love. A child to have. Countries to visit. *You can never know anything in this life.* I closed my eyes and imagined purple twilight over the sanctuary, with nothing but the shake and hum of life all around me.

WINTER IN WISCONSIN

Sally tells Joe they need some aspirin for the grandchild and that he'd better give in and go get some from the Millers. They haven't spoken to the Millers in six months. Not since Pete Miller jumped the curb on Vienna, running his Chevy through their picket fence and into the side of their garage, leaving a red paint scrape and a dent, and no apology.

The fence was one that Joe had built on weekends. It had a gate that closed itself by means of a sash weight tied to a rope, and Sally planted Stanwell Perpetual Old Garden roses in a row along the fence, a variety she special-ordered from a nursery in Connecticut because they reminded her of her grandmother's garden. Pete took out three of the Stanwells, bringing them up from the roots.

"I know we haven't spoken for a while," Sally says, "but they have children's aspirin, and we need to bring the grandchild's fever down."

Joe sits at the kitchen table doing the crossword. Sally walks in a circle, the gold linoleum floor quiet under her feet. She cradles the baby in her arms and touches its forehead. She wears cream-colored polyester pants, a cream-colored sweater, and thin pink slippers with small bows on the front.

"Our grandchild is burning up," Sally says.

"What about the drugstore? Don't they have aspirin?" Joe looks up, his bifocals on the tip of his nose.

"I don't want you driving fifteen miles on icy roads." She walks around humming to the baby and patting its back, and then picks up his crossword and tucks it under her arm.

"What if they won't give me the aspirin?" Joe asks.

"They wouldn't dare. This is a child we're talking about. Tell them we don't want an apology, just aspirin." Then Sally shifts the baby on her hip, and while holding it in one arm, she picks up a dishrag and wipes all the counters.

There is frost in the corners of the windows, and outside it's dark, save the light on their front porch that gives the frosted windows sparkle. Joe stands in front of the bay window looking out, arms crossed and rocking a little from side to side, some from habit and some to Sally's humming.

"I don't like going over there and being the first to make contact, like we're giving in," he says, still looking outside, as if out there he could get lost.

"We're not saying we want friendship, Joe. We just want some aspirin, and then things will go back to the way they've been."

Joe puts his hand on the top of the grandchild's head. Its hair is fuzzy and blond. Its cheeks are rosy and warm. The grandchild has large, brown eyes that look at him with a wisdom that has nothing to do with age. Joe sometimes thinks babies cannot speak because they hold secrets and answers too large for words and understanding. He thinks they carry knowledge from before birth, from somewhere close to God. Joe wishes he could remember what he knew as a child, even remember his mind as a young man.

It's winter in Wisconsin, so Joe puts on his wool coat, hat, gloves, and leather snow boots to walk the three blocks down Vienna. Joe doesn't walk much anymore, but tonight he wants time to think about what he'll say before getting to the Millers.

He worries they'll see him standing on their porch through the kitchen window and keep the lights off and wait for him to leave.

Joe lets the dog out into the backyard so he won't have to walk it later. He takes the sidewalk slowly and carefully, watching his step for ice. He's tall and thin, and holds his arms out at his sides for balance. He doesn't need to fall at a time like this and break something. The neighborhood is quiet, and hard-packed snow crunches under his boots. The homes are one-story and tan brick, almost all the same, and porch lights send long shadows into yards and the street. The snow looks like rock candy—rough-edged, slick, and shiny.

As he gets closer, he sees lights on at the Millers' house. Until a year ago, he and Sally went to their house on Thursday nights to play bridge. They'd sit at a card table in the living room and drink Chablis and eat cheese and crackers. They'd stay up late talking and laughing, telling each other they wouldn't trade these Thursday nights for anything.

A wind blows up the street, and snow drifts over itself and the pavement like shifting sand. Joe pulls up his coat collar and holds it there with both hands as he walks. He thinks maybe he should apologize and get it over with so they can go on being friends in old age. Other friends have already started dying, and he thinks it would be a shame to leave the world with a grudge.

The lights in the Millers' house are warm and yellow. Joe knows Sally misses Barb, their afternoon walks and coffee, and talking about their children. The grudge was more between him and Pete. Pete's vision's been bad. He should have been off the road years ago, but he couldn't face up to it. Pete said he didn't want to lose all his freedoms, didn't want to feel like a man locked to his house, didn't want to feel old and incapacitated. Besides, he told Joe, his own father drove into his nineties.

Pete's accident happened on a bright summer day in July. By the time Joe emerged from the house, Pete was out of the truck, looking at his front fender and the dent in the garage.

"Come for a visit?" Joe said.

"Squirrel shot into the road," Pete said. "Swerved to miss it."

"Time to give it up," Joe said. "I think you know it."

Pete shook his head. A rose bush was tangled and stuck in the grille of his truck. He backed it up, then left the motor running. He placed his fingers between thorns, yanked the bush free, and threw it on the lawn. "Don't tell me what to do, Joe," he said, and got back in the truck and drove off toward town.

Sally and Joe haven't seen Pete driving since. Sally thinks the crash scared him and that he's stopped altogether. Joe thinks he takes the long way out of the neighborhood, avoiding their house at all costs.

Joe steps onto the Millers' front porch. Through the window he sees Barb and Pete watching TV. He recalls a phone conversation with his daughter a few weeks ago. She asked who his friends were, and he told her he wasn't sure. She asked if it was lonely living like that, and he said it wasn't too bad. She told him it was awful he didn't have people to talk to, friends of his own. He told her he wasn't big on having buddies and that he'd been doing all right so far. Standing on the Millers' porch Joe doesn't think it's awful, just awfully unlucky, and rings the bell.

Barb and Pete look at each other, and then Barb gets up and walks to the door. She sees Joe and looks at him from the other side of the glass, her hand over her mouth as if she's about to cry. Then she opens the door.

"Joe," she whispers.

"Barb, I need some aspirin for the grandchild. Sally said you always keep children's aspirin."

"Wait here."

Joe has his face right up to the door, trying to see what they're watching. Inside, Pete turns around, looks at Joe, and turns back. Then he turns off the TV, the lights, and goes into the back of the house after Barb. Joe can hear their voices but can't make out the words.

Joe can see the kitchen counter from where he stands. There's a bottle of ginger ale, a loaf of bread, peanut butter, and orange plastic medicine containers. Pete has diabetes; it came on just after his heart bypass surgery three years ago. He was sixty-two and always ate too much peanut butter. Joe wonders about the condition of Pete's heart.

Joe doesn't think of himself, Sally, Pete, or Barb as being old. But the mind plays tricks, he thinks, and the body is something else. Joe knows their bodies are old enough for surgeries where arteries change to move blood in new ways, affecting the beating of the heart. Maybe it affects the heart entirely, he thinks, in more ways than pumping blood. Or maybe moving things around inside you is a reminder that the heart isn't about emotion or love, but only about keeping you alive.

Joe is cold and wonders what's taking so long. Then Pete comes to the door, hands Joe a Ziploc bag with a bottle of liquid aspirin in it, and says, "This should do it."

"That should do it," Joe says.

"Damn cold out."

"That's winter in Wisconsin."

Pete holds the door open. He wears a wool shirt, slacks, and slippers. They stand there, silent. A dog barks, and there's the hum of traffic from far off. Pete looks past Joe, somewhere over his left shoulder. Their breath looks like smoke against the light and hangs in the air between them. It seems as if Pete has something to say. For a moment, Joe hopes Pete will invite him inside, or tell him to forget about what happened, and he will. All he has to do is say the word.

"Those damn neighbors," Pete says. "They need to put their dog inside in this weather."

Joe puts the bag of aspirin in his pocket. He rubs his gloves together and holds them over his mouth and nose.

"How's Sally?" Pete says.

"Sally's good."

"Barb wants to give her a call. Can she call her?"

"She could have called six months ago. Never said she couldn't."

"I'll tell her then."

Joe reaches in his pocket and holds up the bag of aspirin. "I better get this to the grandchild."

Joe starts down their driveway. When he looks back, Pete is still standing at the door. Joe waves, and Pete nods back. At least he came to the door, Joe thinks. He didn't have to, and he did. As Joe is about to cross the street, Pete calls his name. Joe turns around, and Pete steps onto the porch. In the light his white hair is aglow. He waves Joe toward him.

Joe walks back up the driveway. He looks down and kicks at a loose rectangle of ice.

"Stay here for a minute," Pete says. He goes inside, and then Joe hears him clanking around in the garage. Pete comes back to the door with a pair of large pruning shears.

"I want you to hack off my forsythia bushes there," he says, pointing at the bare bushes lining the edge of his lawn.

"I don't need to do that," Joe says.

"Go ahead; I'll come with you." Joe steps out in his slippers. Joe doesn't want him to slip and fall, or catch cold.

"This isn't necessary, Pete. The past is the past."

"Like hell it is." Pete takes large, slow steps down the driveway with the shears in his hand. Joe walks behind him. Pete steps over a snowbank left from the plow, and walks over the lawn, his weight breaking through its thin, icy crust. Pete doesn't complain of the ice that's probably scraping up his ankles and making them bleed, or the cold that's probably making the bare parts of his legs feel like they're on fire. Joe follows in his tracks, and the snow beneath the surface is soft and slippery. Pete stands in front of a bush. The bushes are four feet tall, and they've been on their lawn for years.

"Barb's not going to like this," Joe says.

"Barb doesn't mind," Pete says. "She wants the air cleared."

Pete hands Joe the shears. Joe takes them and plants his feet into two new holes in the snow in front of the bush.

"Cut it," Pete says. "Cut it down to a stub."

The shears are tight and heavy. Joe opens them and bends down to clip branches near the bottom. He pushes the handles closed with all his strength, and has to open and close them several times. The branches start to bend and snap and fall to the ground.

"That's it," Pete says. "I'm feeling better already."

Joe cuts and cuts, until the bush looks like a small tree stump. Then he moves on to the next, Pete standing beside him the whole time, egging him on, telling him to cut harder, cut lower. Joe feels his body warming up, his face full of color, feels the blood moving through his veins.

"You've got one more," Pete says.

"I can't," Joe says. He breathes heavily, and feels his heart working inside his chest.

"Give me those things." Pete steps over to the last bush and spreads the blades wide. He clips them hard and fast. His nose and ears are bright red, and his eyes water from the cold. When he's finished, he stabs the shears in the snow and leaves them. He smiles and pats Joe on the shoulder.

"I'm frozen," Pete says. "I need to thaw out." They walk back to the driveway through the snow. Pete heads for his house and waves his hand in the air. Joe walks home.

He stands across the street from his own house and looks through the window. Sally sits at the kitchen table with the baby. She talks to it and kisses its forehead. He looks above their house, and stars are bright and clustered in the sky. The stars are always brightest in winter, and he feels like he hasn't seen them in a long time. Orion hangs just above the roof, the line of three stars tilting toward his chimney.

Joe goes around into the backyard. When he unlatches the gate, the dog runs to him and Joe pats his head. He tells him he just saw their old friend Pete. Joe squats down and holds the dog's face in his hands, rubbing his eyes and ears. His mouth is close to the dog's ear, and he says, "I've missed the crabby old bastard." Joe stands and gives the dog a good pat on the side, claps his gloves together, and says, "Let's get inside."

Joe takes his boots off in the hallway. He goes into the kitchen and hands Sally the Ziploc bag.

"Did they put up a fight?"

"No fight. Barb went right into the back of the house, and Pete came back and handed me the aspirin." He hangs his coat over the chair and sets his hat and gloves on the table.

"Did he apologize?"

"He said Barb wants to call you."

Sally holds out the grandchild for Joe to take, and gives it the liquid aspirin with a dropper. She does it the same as she did for their children. Joe cradles his grandchild and remembers what it was like to be a parent to someone so small and new to the world.

Sally nods yes and says, "Good."

They sit in the living room on the old white couch, and Joe rocks the grandchild in his arms. They leave the lamps off, but there is a rectangle of light from the kitchen that comes in on the rug, just far enough to see things in shadow. The baby is warm and soft. It smells like powder and breath. The baby's eyes flutter and its body twitches as it falls into sleep. Joe puts one hand on its chest and can feel its heartbeat, so fast for something so little.

"Feel this—it's going a mile a minute," Joe says. Sally puts her hand on the grandchild's chest, next to his.

"It slows with age," Sally says.

Joe takes his hand off the grandchild's chest and puts it on hers.

"Can you feel it?" Sally says.

The steam heaters come on, clamoring like sailboat masts in a wind. They sit in the dark a while longer, Joe holding the grandchild, Sally's hand on the grandchild's chest, his hand on Sally's chest.

"Can you feel it?" she says.

He can't feel a beat, not a thing but the line of her bra and the rise and fall of her breathing. He closes his eyes and remembers when they were younger, how he'd lay his head on Sally's chest and fall asleep listening to her heart.

"It must be in there somewhere," she says, and puts her hand over his.

Joe wants to tell her his wonder of the things people lose in their lives that shouldn't be lost, and how her hand on his still makes his heart beat faster. Joe leans down and lays his head against Sally's chest. She puts her hand on the side of his face, glides her fingers over his cheek. Her hand is cool, her fingers smooth and gentle. "Oh, Joe," she sighs.

He hears her heart, slow and steady, a deep, resonant beat. He leans into Sally with the grandchild in his arms and imagines them young again, with their own child, their whole lives ahead of them. He thinks this the nicest thing, and knows he could stay this way for a very long time, moving slow with the up and down of breath, the grandchild tiny and warm on his chest. He closes his eyes. The grandchild's breathing is labored, with small airy noises that are wispy and short. They are the small, secret whispers of life.

RETURN IS TO HERE

IT'S JULY AND THINGS are burning—all the trees and brush burning, leaving hanging clouds of smoke like smog in a city, coming in so thick on hot days you can barely see the Sawtooths. I've never witnessed anything like it. I moved to Idaho two years ago from Connecticut. I left the flat and crowded East, looking for something wide open and new. When I drove through this valley, where there are sandy foothills sprinkled green with sagebrush, winding rivers, and mountains that are tall and sharp and purple in the evenings, I stayed. I got a job at a garden center taking care of flowers, shrubs, and trees, and called it good.

There's this thumping noise I can't get rid of that comes up loud in my head at night. I lie in bed poking my finger in my left ear, trying to snuff it out, but then feel the beat on the tip of my finger, and I think for sure there must be a tumor or I'm headed for some imbalance problem and soon I'll be leaning to one side or falling all over the place. It could be the smoke, or it could be intimacy anxiety. There's been a man in my life. We've only been lying around with each other for a month, and sometimes he calls and takes me out to lunch, but I'm giving him part of the blame for the noise in my ear, as if he's brought my heart right up into my head where I hear it all the time. I can't get away from it. Maybe because I haven't felt affection for so long, this is what I get. A loud reminder of my heart, and how it's busting me all up to get going again, get loving again. But I can't put a finger on this man. I can't figure out a goddamn thing except that he likes his dog, guns, my breasts, and ice cream that tastes like peanut butter and chocolate. And I believe he likes them in that order.

His name is Roger, and I have a hard time with that. At thirty, he's too young to be a Roger. Roger is an old man's name, someone who wears brown polyester slacks and has nose hair. When I say his name I sometimes say it twice, Roger Roger, and think of truckers on CB radios. He doesn't see the humor, but I laugh, and he says, Dorie, you're your best audience, you know that?

I tell him I might crack myself up, but I'm still funny, and that maybe he doesn't get my jokes. He says, I get them all right, I get them loud and clear. I tell him he's not a Roger and he says, Who am I then? I say, you're something young and tough like a Rick, Tom, or Dave. He says, I've always been a Roger, so if you start calling me something else we're going to have problems. I say, what kind of problems? He says, problems where I think you have your mind on someone named Rick, Tom, or Dave. I tell him I'll call him Roger then, even though it doesn't fit him, and he says, Call me my name and we should be all set. Then he grabs for my breasts and wants to take it onto the bed. I have mosquito netting hanging from the ceiling that drapes down like a spider web, fine silky white that lets light in in a soft way. I put the netting up for an Africa feel. I've never been, but the pictures of beds in Africa look exotic, restful, private, and pretty.

Roger says, Dorie, let's go into the cocoon and see what's there. He takes me by the hand and holds the netting open for me to pass through. He crawls in and kisses the back of my neck. I like the way he touches me, and so I say, Roger, you've got a way with your hands. He says, Thank you for saying my name. We do it, and then he says he's got to get going. That he's got to feed the dog and get some decent sleep. He slips back out of the netting and dresses.

My friend Jenna tells me I need this, need to get back into the game and have some fun, if for nothing else, to open the heart again. So right off I told Roger I'm not looking for love, just fun. He said, You're not? I said, I'm not what? He said, You're not looking for love? I rolled onto my back and laughed and said, Not right now. When he leaves to go feed his dog, I'm still on the bed naked, and it's so quiet I hear the ticking in my ear again. So I find a cotton ball in the bathroom to plug it up, and lie back down.

I met Roger over a game of darts at Jenna's house. He was quiet and had a straight shot. He got the bull's-eye when he wanted to. When he handed me the darts his hand rested on mine longer than it had to. He touched me every time, soft and easy, and it stirred me up. I could tell how he'd touch my thighs or neck or lower back, and I knew we'd get around to it soon enough.

We got drunk together, and he watched me when I threw darts and watched me when I talked. We were too drunk to drive, so we lay on the lawn in front of Jenna's house. He told me with his old girlfriend it wasn't the right kind of love. I told him no one had come along and gotten to me, so I didn't waste my time. He had a beard. It was after midnight, and warm. He said, I liked you the minute I met you. Then he kissed me, slow and deep, and I knew what was coming my way—a lover. A man fresh from one woman, looking for another to take his mind off things. And at that moment I didn't mind, because he kissed me as if he had been waiting to for a long time.

ROGER TAKES ME OUT to shoot cans with the handgun he keeps behind the seat of his truck. We're parked off an old dirt road that leads up into mountain lakes. I tell him I don't like guns; I've never seen one like this, not up close in real life. He sets up cans on a tree trunk and tells me this spot is good; there isn't anything for the bullets to ricochet off of. I bet this is a test to see if I can stand up to it—shooting a gun. If I don't I can see him calling it quits, I can see him thinking I'm snubbing him, dismissing guns as things for stupid people.

I stand by the truck while he fools with the gun, making sure it's loaded and ready. It's hot and dusty and there's smoke in the air—a sweet, dry smell of burning pine. I slip my foot out of my flip-flop, and the road is sandy and softer than a beach.

"What kind of man are you, Roger?"

"Cattleman," he tells me, and cocks the gun. He has a small scar under his lip, half-buried in his beard. Something he said he got from a bull that could have broken his face if it wanted to. "This office work is for now, for money down the road."

"That's good, that's respectable," I say.

"I know that," he says.

I stand behind his truck when he shoots, and watch from over the hood. The gun going off is loud, and I plug my ears. He hits one can. Then he reloads and hands me the gun. I'm shaky, and he tells me to line my shot up with the sight. I shoot and don't hit a thing but get a ringing in my head. I figure if there's a ricochet then there is, and I'll go down and that will be that. I figure this is a time for me to take chances, all sorts of them, and see what it is to put things on the line. Sex and guns aren't the best way to figure out who you are and where you belong in the world, but I'm trying new things and figure this is a step in the right direction. I figure it's better than sitting home alone or always talking about love with Jenna in her backyard.

I shoot the whole bunch of bullets, eight or maybe ten, and get used to it and come close to one can, nicking the top of the stump.

"Oh, nice try, almost there," Roger says, standing next to me with his arms crossed. When it's over, I keep the gun pointed out toward the stump, and hand it back to him.

"What use is that gun anyway?" I say.

"To shoot cans, and to shoot people before they shoot you." He puts the gun into its case, steps close to me, and touches my neck. "What kind of woman are you, Dorie?"

"I'm a talker," I say.

He pushes the strap of my tank top off my shoulder and licks me.

"If you paid attention, you'd know what's going on, know how to read a situation without talk." He pats me on the butt. We're standing on the driver's side of the truck. He opens the door and reaches in, putting the gun behind the seat.

"I'm not a mind-reader, Roger."

"You sure are pretty," he says, and pulls me toward him by my hips. "If you want to read something, why don't you come closer and read my lips."

I HAVE FRIENDS getting married in Pennsylvania in the beginning of August, and I ask Roger to be my date. He tells me that seems a little serious, but that he'll think about it. I want to know why it seems serious, and he tells me it's not a light thing to fly to a wedding to meet old friends. I ask if maybe he can think of it as friends who have sex, if he can go with me and drink and dance and have a good time, get a little nookie. He tells me he can do that, he can help me out as a friend, and that it would be nice to see Pennsylvania for the first time, maybe do it in a cornfield.

The wedding is in three weeks, and I get a rash. It starts on my belly and moves up over my breasts and down just above my pelvis. It's not a pretty sight, and it itches. I tell Roger this, and he's not pleased, but it doesn't stop him from touching me. He says he had worms as a kid from eating dirt, and that they go away, and that's probably what I have, some kind of worm, maybe from handling flowers and dirt all day in the garden. I tell him I don't have worms, because I don't eat dirt. He says, You have worms all right, and you have to have them yanked out of your butt to get rid of them. I tell him to quit saying I have worms because I don't, and that's a fact. He says, Your friends will be glad to see you, old-red bump Dorie.

THE DERMATOLOGIST wears red shoes, smells like cigarettes, and tells me to relax, I don't have worms. She tells me I've got something no one knows how you get but it just goes away, nothing deadly, nothing that will scar. She gives me a shot of steroids in the hip, and says steroids aren't bad for you, so long as you don't use them all the time, and that they'll get the rash off my skin before the wedding.

I leave feeling good. I get in the car and light myself a cigarette. I go home and wash the car, move some furniture around, and dance to radio music. When Roger comes over I tell him there'll be no more worm comments and that old-red bump Dorie will be clearing up in no time. I feel super, jacked up, and Roger and I have sex all over the place; he tells me he likes the idea of a woman on steroids. He asks me to try lifting him with my legs. I do it, and he gets hot for me and comes back for more.

He sticks around this time, and we lie naked in the cocoon. Above the back of my bed is a window, and there is a full moon shining in on us. He sits up some, his back against the pillows. I lie on my back, my head on his chest, and he holds me, his hands roaming over my stomach and breasts. He asks if I think I could lift the bed with him in it. I tell him I'll do it in the morning. He kisses me on the head and we stay still for a while, wide awake and quiet, the moon shining in and my ear beating like a drum.

In the morning Roger gets coffee and tells me we need to go to the horse races before summer's over, that we should fly to California in September to camp in Yosemite, how when winter comes he'll be calling me at six in the morning to go skiing, and that he's going to leave his toothbrush at my place. I nod to all the ideas and am surprised Roger has thrown us into the future, has thought about seeing me six months down the road.

"What do you mean by all this?" I say.

"What are you getting at?" He sits on my couch in his boxer shorts and drinks coffee. He has a tattoo on his upper arm of a Chinese character that looks like a teapot. I walk over to him and run my fingers over it. He won't tell me what it means, he says, until the time is right.

"You and me?"

"It just means we should do these things because we can."

THREE WEEKS LATER, on a Saturday, Roger and I get on and off a plane together and rent a car. He tells me he's only been on a plane six times in his life, and that he's never liked it. He tells me people should drive, to know how they've gotten to where they're going.

"Can't drive across the ocean," I say. "What if we had to go to Hawaii or Paris?"

"I've never had to go to those places," he says.

"OK," I say. "Was this a mistake?"

"I just never took a jaunt before."

"It's a wedding, Roger."

"Anything that's less than two days and across the country is a jaunt," he says. "Face it, Dorie, you're a jaunter."

We stop at the hotel to change, and Roger wants to do it, but I tell him there's no time. We left early that morning and go back tomorrow evening, and I wish we could stay longer, but I couldn't get time off work. We find our way from the highway onto a rural route that takes us to an old stone house with a sweeping lawn where white chairs are set up, white tents with tables underneath are set for dinner, and a full bar is nestled in a gazebo.

"I could use a beer," Roger says, not moving from his seat in the car. "And a cornfield."

"Later," I tell him. "We have all night."

We step out of the car. He unbuttons his sport coat and shakes out his pant legs.

"I hate suits," he says. "I feel constricted."

"You look very nice," I say, and take his arm in mine. I move us toward a group of people standing on the lawn, all familiar faces I haven't seen in a year. We hug, make small talk about the big wedding day, the beautiful weather, and people shake Roger's hand and tell him how nice it is to meet him. Roger stands with hands in pockets, looking around, listening to talk about places he's never been, reminiscences about times he never knew. People talk about their jobs at banks and ad agencies, about their theater

118

projects and gallery showings, and vacations taken to St. John, Turkey, Vietnam. I smile and nod. I tell them I've been learning a lot about flowers and shrubs in a semi-arid climate. People tell me they think it's great I live in Idaho. Think it's courageous to be so far away and on my own. None of them have been there, aren't sure they could ever live there, but would like to come for a visit. They want to sit in a hot spring, ride a horse, and eat a potato.

My ex-boyfriend from college, Stevens, shows up driving a Mercedes. A big black Mercedes with leather seats. Stevens waves and walks toward us.

"What kind of people do you know?" Roger whispers in my ear.

"I'm sorry," I say.

"It's not your fault," he says.

Stevens, a short New Yorker, wears a dark-gray suit with a blue gingham bowtie. He kisses me on the cheek and introduces himself to Roger.

"Nice car there, Steve," Roger says.

"What are you driving these days, Roger?"

Roger puts his arm on my waist and says, "A pickup with a window that doesn't roll down. Tell me, what do you do to have a honey of a car like that?"

"I write car reviews. And what do you do to have a pickup?"

"None of your business."

"I like that." Stevens laughs. Then he clears his throat and adjusts his glasses. "A man who doesn't give anything away. What do you say we get a drink?"

"You bet," Roger says. Stevens puts his hand on Roger's shoulder like they're old friends, and they walk to the gazebo together.

I stand alone and watch Roger and Stevens at the bar. The trees are full and green. The sunlight comes down in sharp and warm angles, the kind of light that lights up eyes from within and makes people's hair glow on the tops of their heads. It's a perfect evening for a wedding, and I want to be in love.

My old roommate from college, Emily Takamatsu, walks up and tells me I've got one sexy cowboy and that she might have to vacation in Idaho. She wears a black strapless dress and a soft red shawl the color of cranberries. My ear starts ticking, it feels like water in the ear, and I tilt my head to one side to see if that might help.

"He's nice," I say.

"I heard western men are hard to pin down." She holds a pink petit four between two fingers and eats it in two bites. "I heard on NPR people in the West are still accustomed to wide open spaces and have that frontier, exploring side to them. Has he been hard to pin down?"

I light a cigarette, take off my heels, and stand barefoot on the grass. "Not too hard."

"Does he ride horses?" Emily smiles, wiping the corners of her mouth.

"No, but he owns guns, and sometimes he takes me to shoot them."

She holds her drink in front of her lips. "What a turn-on. Well, don't let him keep you in the West. Return back here; we miss you. Or as my Japanese grandfather would say about Japan, 'Emily, return is to here, this where you belong.'" She points at the ground in front of her.

"I miss you too," I say. "Return is to here."

"I want to meet Roger," she says, so we walk over to the gazebo, where Stevens is pretending to shoot a shotgun.

"Forget ducks, Steve, you want to go for elk and big game," Roger says.

Stevens puts his arm around Roger as we step up to them, and he says, "I like this man. No bullshit—this here's the Marlboro Man, ladies."

Roger extends his hand to Emily and says, "I like to call myself full-flavored."

Emily shakes his hand, giggles, and feigns being weak in the knees. "One taste and you never go back?" she says.

"That's right," Roger says, and gives her the raised eyebrow. Then Roger stands next to me and kisses on my neck.

Stevens shakes his head. "Jesus, the man's all beef jerky and blow jobs," he says.

Roger whispers in my ear he thinks Stevens is gay. "He wants me bad," Roger says, and bites my ear. "Only gay men wear bowties."

I turn, my lips right about to touch his. "A lot of people want something they can't have."

"Really," he says. "Is that what it is?" He takes a step back, turns himself in a full circle. "Yeah, all this fucking lack out here—people must be desperate." Then he walks to the bar for another beer.

WE GET BACK FROM Pennsylvania the next night. We don't talk on the ride home from the airport. Roger pulls up in front of my apartment and gets out to hand me my bags from the flatbed of his truck. He sets them on the road and says, "An interesting weekend."

"It's different," I say.

"Did I do all right?"

"It wasn't about that, Roger."

Roger squeezes my arm. "I've got to pick up my dog. He gets pissed when I'm gone. He eats shoes."

I pick up my suitcase and garment bag and kiss him on the cheek. "Thanks."

"OK, Dorie," he says, and walks back to his truck and gets in. I stand in the street and watch his taillights until they're small red dots that disappear around a bend in the dark.

LATE THE NEXT AFTERNOON Roger and I go swimming in the river, and on our way home it's still hot out and so dry it seems you could spit and it would evaporate midair. The heat has been with us for weeks, heat that doesn't belong in mountain towns in August. And there have been so many fires. None so close that I have seen flames, but the ever-present haze leaves me with a cough and red eyes. There are so many fires in the West there's nothing to be done until snow and rain come fall.

"You know, I like this life here," I say.

"Good," he says. "It's a good life."

"I'm sorry about the wedding."

"You don't need to talk." He puts a finger over his lips.

"I didn't bring you as some token Idaho cowboy."

"Not today, Dorie. I'm tired from the sun and have too much on my mind."

"Like what?"

"Some things I keep private."

We're wet and sunburned. The land is dry and brown, and we drive through a canyon that's steep and striated. My window's down, the only window that goes down, and the hot air blows in on us. I'm drowsy.

"What are we doing?"

"Tomorrow, Dorie. I'll come over tomorrow night, and you can talk all you want."

My arm's hanging out of the window when a pebble or bug or something whacks my hand at seventy miles per hour; it hits me like a bullet and stings. My eyes get wet so I shut them. I feel foolish.

ROGER DOESN'T COME OVER the next night so I can talk all I want. He doesn't call the next day either. Finally, after three days, Roger comes over. He comes to get what's his—a video that's overdue, a CD, and while he's at it he picks up his T-shirt and toothbrush. I figure if I don't say something now I might not see him again. While he's rooting out his CD I say, "Can you stay a minute?"

"I've got to get going, I have things to do."

I can't believe he's just going to walk out of here like he never knew me in the first place. Just walk out and find someone else who can have fun and keep her heart out of it. Although I know that's not all that's going on here. He's half out the door, holding everything he came for.

"I have something to say," I say.

"Do I need to sit down for this?"

"I don't think so, but could we shut the door?"

He shuts the door and waits. I want to ask about the horse races, California, and skiing. I want to ask what he wants, because I don't really want it to end. I just started feeling something for the first time in a long time, and I'm not ready for it to stop. I know it's selfish, and that we're not a good match, but we're good enough for now.

"I wish things were different," I say.

Roger shrugs, looks at the doorknob. "They are the way they are, Dorie."

"Roger."

"I like you," he says. "I'll see you around."

THREE WEEKS GO BY, and no Roger. I don't see him around. The beating in my ear is alarming. I think for sure a doctor is needed. I'm afraid my heart is going to bust out of my head. I can't sleep, and I think about Roger more than is healthy. I call him twice, but he doesn't call back. I drive by his house late at night looking for his truck, but it's never there. I feel crazy, like some sick stalker. Then I come home and crawl into bed, my pretty bed with mosquito netting. I cry a little for us not working out, even though I'm not sure where we could have gone. Then I cry harder for wanting love so badly I'd try to squeeze it out of Roger, and for not understanding what the hell *return is to here* means, even though I can't stop thinking about it. Return is to where? I don't know where I belong.

The nights are cooling off, and the air feels tighter. I know the trees will be turning soon, reds and oranges like paint, like nothing you'd think a tree could turn in September. And then snow and rain will come, cover us in clouds, and put out some of the fires.

I wake at three in the morning to the woman upstairs walking on hardwood floors. It sounds as though she keeps falling, or tripping over furniture in the dark. It goes on and on, so I walk upstairs barefoot in my pajamas and stand outside her door to listen and figure it out. I'm about to knock to ask her to keep it down when I hear voices, a male and female, and the sounds of bodies settling into a bed. The bed must be close to the door, because I hear them clearly, their voices carrying out to where I stand in the hallway a good three feet from the door. They talk about blueberry pancakes in the morning and taking a hike and fishing in the river. Then there's the sound of kissing, and the women lets out a sigh like I've never heard before. It isn't a tired sigh, but something high and airy, as if she has everything she needs. It is a sigh of contentment. I take the stairs down to my apartment trying to mimic the sigh, but I can't find the right pitch, or the right release of air.

HEARTBREAK HOTEL

"I WANT TO TELL YOU something heartbreaking," my daughter Lindsey says. We're playing Heartbreak Hotel. We've played it in the car since she was ten, old enough to know what heartbreak and heartache is about. It's not a win-lose game. It's a get-to-know-you game. Lindsey drives. We're on Highway 20 near Picabo, a two-laner through high desert. It's June in southern Idaho, an afternoon when the air is so hot the heat hovers over the road in a blur. Sagebrush and more sagebrush sprinkle the brown plains and mountains with green. The sky blooms blue above us.

"It broke my heart when I was thirteen and realized I wouldn't be an astronaut," she says.

"But you were a successful space cadet," I say.

"Very funny, Dad." She gives me the sideways eye. She is a pretty girl and looks younger than her thirty-five years. She has black-as-night hair and freckles like tiny constellations on her face. I am proud she is my daughter.

We are on our way to Boise, where she has a new apartment and a new job as curator of the Boise Art Museum. There is a welcome reception for her in the main gallery at seven tonight. We started in Boston, and this is our sixth and last day on the road. What am I doing here? I've never driven across the United States, and how many times in your life do you get to spend a week alone with one of your children getting to know her as an adult by traveling roads across your very own country? I turn the air conditioner down to sixty-four degrees.

"I want to tell you something heartbreaking," I say.

Lindsey reaches between the seats for something in the back and pats her hand around like a blind person looking for a wall.

"Hands on the wheel," I say. "What do you need?" The car is hers, a silver Volkswagen Jetta.

Lindsey comes back around. "Hands are on the wheel," she says. "I need my driving cap."

She's insisted on wearing a driving cap this whole week. It's kelly green and knitted and the ugliest thing I've ever seen. I reach back, find it, hand it to her.

"What is it with this hat?" I ask. "It's ninety-nine degrees on the road."

"It keeps me alert," she says, and adjusts the hat and scratches her forehead.

"Because it makes your head itch?"

"Dad, just say your heartbreak."

I was going to tell her it breaks my heart I never got to move about like she does, never got to follow my passions and take risks, but instead I say, "It breaks my heart to see you wear that hat."

Then hail comes out of nowhere. The sky is blue one minute, and then ice rocks are bamming the roof, the hood, and pinging off the windshield, steaming up the road.

"Jesus," she says. "Good thing I have my hat on."

"Pull over, Lindsey," I say. "Don't get excited."

She eases onto the shoulder. I roll my window down a slice. The air smells like hot wet blacktop and spearmint from the damp sagebrush.

"Should we get out?" she says. "Feel it?"

"If you want to get knocked out," I tell her. "I'll be in here."

The hail shrinks to pebble size in minutes but still falls strong and covers the ground like confetti. Lindsey opens the door and slides out. One small hail ball flies in on the leather seat, and I pick it up and roll it between my fingers until it melts.

When she comes back inside, her hat and face are wet and shiny.

"I have something heartbreaking to tell you," she says.

"I'm all ears," I say, and hand her a tissue from the glove compartment. She wipes her cheeks and chin, then bites her thumbnail. I know this habit of hers. She's holding in her heartbreak, and has a downward kind of smile like she's apologizing for what she's about to say.

TWO HOURS EARLIER we made a lunch stop in Arco to get a hamburger and milkshake at Pickle's Place. Then we went to the first plant to use atomic power for electricity, where my maternal uncle Don Pettitt had been a physicist in the 1950s. There were a couple lightbulbs lit up as proof, and a chalkboard behind a Plexiglas cover on which he and ten other scientists had signed their names. In 1951 they powered a lightbulb. In 1955 they lit up the whole town, the first city in the world to be powered by nuclear energy under Eisenhower's Atoms for Peace program. Now it's a museum.

Lindsey and I stared at the lightbulbs, their little filaments bright like the sun inside the glass. The rest of the place had painted cement floors and walls in gunmetal gray. Dull and institutional. It felt like we were in a prison, and the air smelled like chalk and cold metal desks. There were a lot of large contraptions with buttons, levers, numbers, and yellow signs everywhere announcing danger, as if touching something might end life on Earth. They looked like time machines.

"I'd get inside one of those and go to Greece, wear a white toga and flat sandals and have someone braid my hair every day," Lindsey said, "then feed me figs and lamb and red wine."

"First, I'd go to the Civil War, straight to Gettysburg," I said. "July 1, 1863. I'd live in Paris, drink with Hemingway and Fitzgerald, and write novels. Then I'd go watch Babe Ruth play baseball."

"Busy," she said.

"There are only so many things you can be in one life. I wish there was more time to be all the other mes."

"All the other yous?" she said, with air quotes.

"I had dreams. Being a foot doctor wasn't my number-one passion in life. Did you know I had a parakeet named Budge when I was twelve, and for years all I wanted to do was be an avian vet? Did you know I wrote three novels in college, all of which I burned one drunken night after Janice Hansen dumped me senior year?"

"I didn't know that," Lindsey said.

"Now you do. Now you know some secret information about your dear old dad."

She nodded as if in thought, but didn't seem impressed or particularly surprised. I hadn't told many people, other than my wife, any of those things. I never wanted my girls to know I often wished I'd veered off the straight and narrow path to follow my heart. I was practical, and when you have a wife and kids, a house, car, and food to pay for, risks aren't wise or welcomed.

A man with thick-soled black shoes was being loud to our right near the lightbulb exhibit.

"Are you kidding, are you serious?" He wiped his hand over his mouth and shook his head. "All those brains, and all they came up with was how to light a lightbulb?"

I moved toward this man. I tended to move toward people in a rage.

"I'm not a physicist," I said, "but nuclear electricity was one of the most efficient forms of power we've ever known. These lightbulbs are brilliant, if you think about it."

He turned to me, his shoes squishing on the floor, his lips parted. His head jerked back. "Are you a tour guide?"

Then it occurred to me he might be a man who didn't want

to think about *it* or anything else.

Lindsey stood by the machine with her arms crossed and her head cocked to one side. She'd seen me approach people before. My own father was a man with a temper, and I'd spent my youth trying to reason with him and calm him down. He'd go off about any small thing—a candy wrapper that didn't look right, if the washing machine made a funny noise, or whatever he felt like raging about to compensate for his own confusion and self-hatred, and for all the pent-up anger he had about things he'd wanted to do but never did. He didn't change jobs, or even choose a profession. He was a plumber, because his father was a plumber. He never lived outside of Lowell, Massachusetts, or traveled overseas. But his brother chose to go to college and became a physicist. His brother lived in places like Arco, Idaho, and Osaka, Japan, and then came home to teach at MIT. But my father was a stuck man, and an angry man, and I vowed I'd never be like him.

"No, no tour guide," I said. "But my uncle is Don Pettitt up there." I pointed to the blackboard.

"Big whoop," the man said. He stared at me, strained his eyes wide. He waited for my next move. He had large face pores and fish lips.

"Are we in junior high?" I said. "I'm sorry. It's an incredible lightbulb. I didn't mean to disturb you." I walked back toward Lindsey; I didn't want to look at him anymore.

"Nice one, Mr. Science," the man said, and followed me.

I waved my hand in the air, a brush-off goodbye.

"Hey, Mr. Science," he said, "why's the tour over so fast?"

"Dad," Lindsey said in a low voice, "you've got to stop doing this."

"Who are you, anyway?" the man asked.

"My daughter and I are just passing through," I said.

The man stood in front of us with his arms crossed over his chest. He looked at Lindsey, then me, then back at Lindsey.

"You don't look related," he said. "Are you sure this isn't your young girlfriend?"

A generator clicked on and hummed loudly.

"You're gross," Lindsey said to him. "I'm out of here," and she walked for the exit.

I turned to follow her, and the man stepped in my path. "I bet that's your BMW from California in the parking lot. I can tell by how you dress," he said.

"All right," I said, and looked down at my clothes. I didn't know how someone who drove a BMW dressed. I didn't have a BMW.

"It's the Oxford shirt and loafers," he said. "I bet you loaf around and then get into that fancy box and zoom around thinking you're better than other people, don't you?"

"You're a real brain surgeon," I said. "Sherlock Holmes. I'm sorry I approached you. Now excuse me."

I walked around him slowly. He seemed like the kind of guy who might body-check me or grab my collar.

As I was about to leave the building, he yelled, "Hey, Mr. Manners."

I turned around. He stood in the same place, arms still crossed, watching me. "I'll be on the road today," he said and winked. "I'll be looking for you."

THE HAIL DOESN'T LAST LONG. It never does. But the air is different—it's lighter and cleaner. There's blue sky all around except for right above us, and it feels like we're under the shadow of a maple tree. Lindsey doesn't give up her heartbreak, and I don't want to push it. I'm grateful to learn about my daughter in these ways, but her heartbreaks seem negligible. I respect her challenges, and I know everyone carries their own brand of hurt, but she is so lucky: She's young, lives her life according to her passions, and I imagine carries little regret, if any. I carry little regret myself, but what I would have given for the choices and freedoms she has.

"Why don't I drive?" I ask, and we switch seats.

I pull onto Highway 20, shift into fifth, and get up to sixty-five in under a minute. "Nice car," I say.

"That guy in Arco was creepy," Lindsey says.

"Forget about him," I say.

"Why do you need to talk to people like that?"

"I don't know." I tap the steering wheel. "Maybe I feel like I can change their minds about something."

"You're lucky that asshole didn't have a gun," she says.

I miss my own bed, my wife, my space. My ass hurts from sitting in this car all day every day for six days, and I'm ready to go home, but a thought crosses my mind that has been crossing my mind a lot lately—I am getting old, I am sixty-five, and I might not get to spend time with my children like this for much longer. I have been telling myself to look around, be aware, listen more closely. Be thankful. Be glad for the life I've been given and have created.

Ten miles down the road we stop at a Stinker station, and I fill up. We go in for bathrooms, pretzels, and Diet Cokes, and when we come out, the man from the museum is sitting in the backseat of our car with his seatbelt on. He smiles and waves.

"Is this really happening?" Lindsey asks. "Jesus. This is a joke, right? We have three hours to drive, check into the hotel, and get ready for tonight. This cannot happen right now."

I open the door and say, "You need to get out of this car. This isn't a BMW."

"Mr. Manners," he says, "I missed you."

"No way," Lindsey says. She goes back into the store, and I see her talking to the clerk and pointing at us.

"I bet," I say. "What are you doing?"

"Listen," he says. "I'm just loafing around." He lifts up his foot and has tan Docksiders on.

"Those shoes will give you bunions, so you better get out and buy another pair."

"Nice try," he says.

"I'm a foot doctor," I tell him. "Your feet are probably already red and swollen at the edges. You'd be better off with those gummy geriatric shoes."

A PA system clicks on, and a woman says, "Man in the silver Volkswagen. Man, you best move along or the authorities will be involved."

He bends down and takes off his shoes. His feet are red and swollen at the edges.

"What else?" he asks. "Do you know how my cotton polyester shirt will affect my skin? Do you know why I have a bald spot on the back of my head but thick hair everywhere else? Do you know why my leg twitches when I fall asleep?"

"No," I say, "because I'm a foot doctor."

"Isn't that exciting?" he says and runs his hand over his bald spot.

Lindsey comes out, followed by the attendant, who looks eighteen and wears checkered high-tops and a fluorescent pink T-shirt with a bright-yellow lightning bolt in the center.

The attendant walks to our car, looks at me, and says, "I'm Paivi, sir, and this has never happened before." Then she looks at the man in my car and says, "Dude, you can't sit in other people's cars."

The man is still looking at his feet and then sets the shoes aside on the seat. "Why do you call him sir and me dude? This man is my brother," he says, nodding at me. "These two are just having a bad day."

"We are not related. This man is a crazy stalker with road rage," Lindsey says.

"How did you get here?" I ask him.

"I've got my ways," he says.

Two RVs from Wyoming pull in, and Paivi says, "Oh, my God," and rolls her eyes. "I hate RVs. I have to go deal with these road hogs. Come tell me if you want me to call the cops." She walks back into the store.

Lindsey looks at both of us. "I have to get to Boise. I have a new job and a fancy reception to attend, and neither of you better screw this up for me. This is all I have. I don't have a husband, I don't have kids, but I do have a good job, and I don't want to lose it. If you won't get the hell out, then you're coming with us." She sits in the car and waits. Then the man in my backseat settles in and waits. Lindsey purses her lips and twists her hands together, as if this man were a small, harmless child throwing a tantrum who needs to be ignored. The man sighs and nods at me as though we best get going, quit wasting time.

"Lindsey, honey, get out of the car. What if this man has a knife or a gun?"

"Mr. Manners," he says, "I don't have anything but these shoes. Nobody ever committed a crime with a shoe."

"The hell they haven't." I go around and open the back door, grab his shirt at the chest, and try to pull him toward me, but he doesn't budge. I repeat this three times, and he's sturdy as a block of cement, so I touch his shirt and pants for weapons and don't feel anything except a wallet. He doesn't flinch or look at me the whole time. He smells moldy, like something wet that never dries.

"Come on, Dad," Lindsey says. "I have my pocketknife. I'll stab the motherfucker if he gets funky."

"He's already funky."

"I can hear you," the man says.

"Good, he can hear us," Lindsey says. "Now let's go.

I am surprised by how unconcerned she is, oblivious of the dangers that lurk. Or maybe it's this fearlessness that allows her to take the risks she does.

"Get in the car, Dad."

The man nods yes.

"This is crazy," I say. "I'm your father. I'm supposed to protect you."

"Maybe it's too late. Maybe I'm too old for that," she says. "Let's go."

It seems as if these two laconic figures—my beloved inscrutable daughter and this menacing inscrutable stranger are both grimly, silently, patiently waiting for me as if they've struck a deal—have forged something of an alliance against me and my ways of thinking.

"You're never too old," I say.

"That's sweet," the man says. "I wish I had a father who gave a crap."

I get into the car. "Tell me your name and where we are dropping you off." I look in the rearview mirror. He's smiling and has a far-off look.

"I don't know yet," he says.

"You don't know your name?" I say.

"Or where I'm going," he says.

Lindsey takes off her hat and holds it in her lap. "Deep," she says. "Mysterious."

"It is a deep and mysterious world, young lady," he says.

She loops her pinky through one of the knit holes in the hat.

"Did you make that thing?" I ask.

"Just drive, would you?" She exhales loudly and tilts her head against the headrest, her eyes toward the ceiling. It's as though she has a near-desperate need to get to her destination, a need whose urgency I can't quite understand, but that has made her reckless.

"I'm not the bad guy here, honey—take it easy."

She lifts her knee and bangs her foot down on the floorboard three times.

I put my hand on top of her knee. She's crying.

"Can we just go, please?"

I turn around. "Listen, man. You're upsetting my daughter. Think you could leave?"

"I don't care about him," Lindsey says through a hiccup. "This has nothing to do with him."

"What is this?" I say.

"I don't want to live in Boise."

"Oh boy," the man says from the backseat.

"Would you shut up?" I say.

The RV motors rumble back to life—summer vacationers with bicycles and kayaks attached to their vehicles. In the mirror, I see the man check his watch as though he has somewhere to be.

"It's been a long trip. You're tired and nervous." I put my hand on her shoulder, but she flinches it away.

"Get going," she says. "I don't want to be stuck behind those vacation homes on wheels."

"This is your last chance to get out," I say to the man. "I'm a horrible driver, and your life is at risk."

"I'm very comfortable, thank you," he says.

I start the engine and pull onto the road. We need to make time and hope for the best with the stranger in the backseat.

"I've heard great things about Boise," I say to Lindsey.

"I'm tired of moving, and of being far away and alone." She wipes at her eyes with the palms of her hands. "I want a redo."

"This is a redo," I say.

She's been so many places, done so many things. Boston, Seattle, Vietnam, Argentina. Teacher, photographer, Red Cross worker, French translator, and now an art curator. She's had a wonderful, adventurous life, and I tell her that all the time. But it seems she has no idea where she belongs, and I know it breaks her heart to be moving through the world alone, searching for a reason to stay in one place, looking for someone to anchor her. The heartbreak of loneliness is a real ache and something I can't fix for her.

"A redo to have made a different choice years ago to stay put and make a life in one place with someone," she says.

"With someone who?"

"I don't know," she says. "Maybe Mark or Jason or Peter would have worked out if I hadn't been so brash and could have been more accommodating, made more compromises."

"Accommodating. Like hell."

"I'm not impossible."

"Never said you were. You have standards. Keep them. Look at all the risks you've taken. Risks I never took, risks my father never took that soured him on life. I admire you for that. You've seen and done more than most people my age."

"By myself."

"You only have yourself."

"I hate that saying. I bet even this guy has more than himself."

She points her thumb toward the backseat.

"I have a twelve-year-old son named Jacob," he says, "and a cat named Ndugu."

"*See?*" Lindsey says.

"Quit feeling sorry for yourself," the man says. "So what, you don't have a boyfriend? So what, you live alone? You have a family, you have a job, you have a Volkswagen, and I bet you went to college and have a friend or two. Boise's not a bad place. They have restaurants and movies."

Lindsey rolls down her window and leans her head out. The desert is flat, with silvery sagebrush and cheatgrass as yellow and dry as hay. Beyond are brown and chiseled mountains. The heat pushes in. It is dry, like sauna heat. A tissue in the cupholder rises and flies out the window like a ghost.

"Good-bye, tissue," Lindsey says. "Fare thee well."

We are ten miles from Highway 84, which will take us west to Boise. I drive us down into a valley that's burned out, charred black, and smells like ash. A cigarette thrown out the window? A spark from an exhaust pipe? Lightning? It is a scarred and barren landscape. It is ignitable. It is unforgiving. There is nowhere to hide.

The air makes a sealing sound as Lindsey rolls up her window. "It is so hot," she says. "And dead. I might as well move to the goddamn moon."

"Don't go to the moon," I say.

"Fine, Venus. Maybe I can find a lover on Venus."

She asks us all the time why she's alone, why she's not found a man to marry and with whom to have children, but we don't know. Nothing is a given. Not even the love between a parent and a child. I wonder if I was lucky to have met my wife, or if I simply made a choice and stuck with it; or maybe it was both, because I am happy, and I still love my wife, and there is nowhere I'd rather be.

"It will work out," I say. "You'll be a top-notch curator. They need you. And you're not alone. You'll never be alone."

"You don't know that."

"I'll bet on it."

"The moon would be cold anyway," the man says from the backseat. "And you'd have to float everywhere and eat dried foods."

Lindsey laughs.

"There you go," the man says.

"Is Boise your heartbreak?" I ask.

"Partly," she says. "But mostly it's being alone."

"Heartbreak?" the man asks.

Lindsey turns to look at him. "Tell us your heartbreak."

I watch him in the mirror. His eyes dart back and forth, and he bobs his head a little. "Is moving to Boise and not having a boyfriend really so heartbreaking it's making you cry?" he asks.

"I have every right to be sad about whatever I want," she says. "My feelings are mine."

The man unbuckles his seatbelt and leans forward between the seats. I put my hand on the phone. I've had my cell dialed on 911 and ready to go, resting on my left thigh, but there's not been any reception until now.

"You invite heartbreak," he says. "You set yourself up for it."

"Please sit back," I say. I get a whiff of mothball and dust.

"Is this a habit of yours?" Lindsey asks. "Hobo philosopher?"

"It gets me where I need to go," he says. "Everybody's going somewhere. Be happy you have somewhere to go, and that there are people who know where you are in the world. I haven't seen my son in ten years and my parents are dead and that's just the way it is."

"Well, I don't know where I'm going," Lindsey says. "I'm sorry about your son and your parents."

"Thank you," he says. "I appreciate that."

We drive on without talk between us. We sail down a long hill and then the land flattens. There are green fields of potatoes. There are cattle and scruffy horses. There are weathered wooden rail pasture fences that lean forward and backward, warped, as though a good wind could blow them over. The sky is big. I can see a long way. Hundreds of miles south are the Owyhee Mountains, and to the east and west are plains, and deep cuts where the land drops into the Snake River canyon, where the surface of the earth breaks into crevices and cracks left behind from the elements wearing her down, reshaping her, making her to shift and change, shift and change.

Fast food and gas stations and minimarts are ahead.

"My stop's up here," he says. "The gas station with the Arby's."

I pull into the lot and park.

He steps out and shuts the door. He raps on Lindsay's window with his knuckles. She rolls it down, and for a moment I think he has something to give her, like a business card or a piece of candy.

He taps his finger on his temple over and over. "You think too much. You're going to Boise, kid, and that's the way it is. Don't spend so much time wishing for things you don't have. You'll get what you're supposed to get."

The sun is low and directly in front of us, streaming through the windshield. The sunlight washes a copper glow over the dry, brown desert that's flat as a plate to the west. The man cups one hand over his eyebrows and looks out toward the highway into the light. "Straight that way. It's as simple as that. A new start. A second or third or fourth chance. Lucky you." The man bangs on the roof of the car with his hand, twice. "Lucky you," he says again, and then turns and walks through the filling station into the Arby's.

I think, yes, lucky her. How many times do you get to start over in this life? How many?

Lindsey looks into the setting sun, and so do I. It lights her face. Her hair glows like it's on fire, and her brown eyes become translucent-like; I see lines of orange, like tiger stripes, deep inside them. She's my girl. She'll come through. She'll be all right. And I know she knows, as I know and as my father knew, that you just keep going. You keep going. It's all you can do.

ACKNOWLEDGMENTS

These stories have appeared previously (sometimes in different form) in the following publications: "Sanctuary," *Potomac Review*, summer 2016; "Man Is the Measure of All Things," *Kenyon Review Online*, summer 2016; "Return Is to Here," *Failbetter*, May 2014; "How Far to Go," "All These Lovely Boys," and "Love Is No Small Thing," *Violet Magazine*, April 2014; "Heartbreak Hotel," *Five Chapters*, July 2013; "Love Is No Small Thing," *Cincinnati Review* 8, no. 1 (2011); "All These Lovely Boys," *Hobart*, April 2010; "I'll Tell You What," *Pleiades* 30, no. 1 (2010); "The Genius of Love," *Florida Review* 34, no. 1 (2009); "What Will Make This All Right," *Kenyon Review* 31, no. 2 (2009); "Winter in Wisconsin," *Cimarron Review*, no. 161 (2007); "These Things Happen," *Gettysburg Review* 18, no. 3 (2005).

Thank you to the journals and editors who published each of these stories, and to the Boise State University MFA program, The Cabin, Idaho Writers in the Schools Program, Vermont Studio Center, La Muse, Kenyon Review Writers' Conference, The Tickner Writing Fellowship at Gilman School, Bread Loaf Writers' Conference, and Sewanee Writers' Conference for time and support.

An enormous thank you to Michael Griffith, for believing in my book and making each of these stories stronger, and to James Long, Lee Sioles, Susan Murray, Erin Rolfs, and the team at LSU Press for their hard work.

I am deeply grateful for my teachers and mentors along the way for passing down their love of language and story, and for making me a writer: Bob Cole, Robert Olmstead, Colum McCann, David Lynn, Sergei Lobanov-Rostovsky, Nancy Zafris, Mitch Wieland, Janet Holmes, Martin Corless-Smith, and Ron Carlson.

With great appreciation and affection for my friends and advisors who helped shape many of these stories, and encouraged and nudged me forward at the most important times: Tamara Shores, Heather Parkinson Dermott, Christian Winn, Jennifer Bryan, John Wang, Jen Michalski, Laura van den Berg, Jenniffer Gray, Alyssum Wier, PJ Mark, Marya Spence, my Boise, Japan, Baltimore and Lancaster writing communities, and my Kenyon tribe.

With so much love and thanks to my parents and sister, Erin, for always telling me to keep writing and to never give up. You have taught me that love is no small thing; it is big; it is important; it is everything.

CPSIA information can be obtained
at www.ICGtesting.com
Printed in the USA
LVOW08s1356130217
524112LV00001B/73/P